NANOWIRED

By

Paul M. Valliant

Order this book online at www.trafford.com
or email orders@trafford.com

Most Trafford titles are also available at major online book retailers.

Note for Librarians: A cataloguing record for this book is available from Library
and Archives Canada at www.collectionscanada.ca/amicus/index-e.html

Printed in Victoria, BC, Canada.

ISBN: 978-1-4269-0445-5 (Soft)
ISBN: 978-1-4269-0446-2 (Dust)
ISBN: 978-1-4269-0446-2 (e-book)

*Our mission is to efficiently provide the world's finest, most comprehensive
book publishing service, enabling every author to experience success.
To find out how to publish your book, your way, and have it available
worldwide, visit us online at www.trafford.com*

Trafford rev. 9/17/2009

 www.trafford.com

North America & international
toll-free: 1 888 232 4444 (USA & Canada)
phone: 250 383 6864 • fax: 812 355 4082

DEDICATION

To forensic investigators who solve crimes

FOREWORD

Human civilization has fostered the belief there are intrinsic "goods" and intrinsic "bads". Modern behavioural neuroscience, with the tools to directly observe the brain when a person engages in moral decision-making, has shown that "good" versus "bad" reasoning is simply another brain function. This realization that morality or correctness of behaviour is relative and not absolute has begun to unravel foundations of law, social structure, and the understanding of the human self.

In "Nanowired" Dr. Paul Valliant has crafted a complex literary presentation of the dilemma of a society where the thoughts and actions of the "police" and the "criminals" converge into frightening similarity. Cast within an international setting where political intrigue and disregard for life is punctuated only by financial gain, "Nanowired" follows the progression of Emerald Lee as he changes from a stereotyped caricature of a sociopath to a complex character whose final act challenges the reader's appreciation for what actually controls conscience and morality.

"Nanowired" is exciting in content and captivating in composition. It is also one of the most disturbing novels I have read. Paul Valliant's sagacious style of embedding the ambiguities of "right" and "wrong" within a text of succinct dialogue and intermittent introspection can seduce the reader into the complacency this is just another story. However, the message of "Nanowired" evokes one of the most important questions of human existence. Is there an intrinsic morality within all human brains and if there is do we have the technology to control it?

Dr. M. A. Persinger
Full Professor
Behavioural Neuroscience and Psychology
Laurentian University

PREFACE

In this fictional novel, Detective Brown is cast as the protagonist whose approach toward justice is cast in his crime control model. Detective Brown finds himself in conflict with lawyers whose model of due process interferes with his attempt to incarcerate the criminal element of New York. In his work, Detective Brown encounters Emerald Lee, a terrorist who is wounded at the scene of his latest crime. Emerald Lee is incarcerated but later sent to the Bingham Neurosurgical Centre to remove a blood clot suffered from a bullet wound during his arrest. In preparation for his surgery, Emerald Lee encounters medical specialists who evaluate him. Unknown to Lee, nanotechnology is used during the surgical procedure to remove his homicidal aggressive behaviour. This fictional novel reflects on the early pioneering research of neurosurgical specialists who utilized electrode implantation and electrical stimulation to thwart aggressive behaviour. In this novel, nanowiring is explored as the futuristic technique of controlling aggressive psychopaths.

CHAPTER 1

The morning sun was creeping above the trees on the east side of Toronto. People were moving in the streets, a new day was coming to life in the crowded city. Employees in the CBB newsroom on 100 Bloor Street were preparing their equipment for the 7 a.m. newscast. Karen Jacks adjusted the microphone attached to the lapel of her dark blue jacket as she looked up at the camera.

"Today is going to be a warm one with the temperature going to 20 degrees Celsius. Now, for the top news of the morning. Dr. Jobin an eminent environmentalist was shot dead in his downtown Forest Hill home. According to the report, he was killed this morning while reading the early edition of the newspaper. I am going to turn you over to Michael Smith a news correspondent on location at Dr. Jobin's residence. Michael can you hear me? This is Karen Jacks! I understand you are at the scene right now. Could you tell us what happened?" The camera focused in on the tall handsome newscaster.

"Thank-you Karen. You can see from the number of police milling around here, Dr. Jobin's death is of some concern. As you know Karen, Dr. Jobin was on the Board of Directors with Panax Corporation. From what I can gather at this time, police are saying Dr. Jobin was killed by a single bullet. I just talked with Detective Sergeant James in the homicide division with the Metro Police Service. He preferred not to be interviewed but indicated he will make a statement later today. From the appearance of the crime scene, I was informed this doesn't look like an accidental shooting. Initially, there was some talk a hunter was in the Ravine this morning shooting at deer. Police however, believe the shooting was not accidental. As you can see from the close up, the bullet penetrated the glass pane and killed Dr. Jobin while he sat at his kitchen table. The police are attempting to retrieve some clues from the crime scene. They are searching the east side of the property near the stone wall. It appears the gunman took his deadly shot from about 50 yards from the house. From what I have gathered, the police are combing the grounds for bullet casings. The Forensic Unit is sweeping the area. No one has been allowed to enter the yard because they don't want the crime scene contaminated. There are two criminal analysts here, looking at the evidence. They are attempting to piece this together so they can make some sense of the homicide. That's about it for now Karen. I'll have more about this incident on the update at 12:00 noon," said the newscaster.

"That was Michael Smith live from Forest Hill. We will have more news about the killing later in the day. This is Karen Jacks from the CBB network."

Jonathan Richardson, president of Panax Corporation depressed the button on the teleconverter and the monitor faded. He sat in silence in the back seat of his black limousine as it sped along the Don Valley Parkway. The vice-president of Panax Corporation had been murdered. An emergency meeting with the board members would take place as soon as he arrived at his office. He would telephone the firm contracted to provide security to his agency. Twenty-four/seven protection would be offered to board members and the administrative staff at Panax Corporation. Surveillance cameras would be installed on the homes of all employees as an added measure. Dr. Jobin's death would create some panic at the Panax Corporation.

Jonathan Richardson would personally contact the police chief at the Metro Police Service and ask for an update on the investigation. The directors of the Panax Corporation held powerful positions in the city. He would contact the mayor's office and arrange a personal meeting. Jonathan Richardson would demand the city bring in its best forensic investigators to solve Dr. Jobin's homicide. He thought back to the development of Panax Corporation. The company had been started twenty five years prior as a private organization to deal with the complaints against Industrial firms intent on polluting the environment. With the generous donations from well known North American philanthropists, the Panax Corporation had gained notoriety. High profile lawyers had offered their services pro bono and taken the North American Industrialists to court. The civil litigation had proven costly to the Industrial firms. Many were forced into bankruptcy protection whereas others had to undertake costly measures to minimize the impact of the hazardous wastes. Jonathan Richardson was having an impact on the environment. Toxic waste had been reduced by 60 percent and the Panax Corporation was making significant gains in the Industrialized world.

He reflected back on the inception date of the Panax Corporation. It was shortly after his meeting with Dr. Nokama the renowned West Coast biologist, Panax Corporation was created. Jonathan Richardson's affiliation with the west coast activists had helped the Panax Corporation gain notoriety in its infant stages. He reflected back on the early years. Jonathan Richardson had chained himself to a 200 year old Douglas fir in an attempt to block the logging firm from decimating the ancient forest in Clayoquot Sound. He had been there in the beginning and suffered physical and emotional abuse at the hands of the Industrialists in their attempt to gain control of parkland. He had come a long way since those early days. Through his work, he had made a significant impact on the British Columbia logging firms.

After completion of his law degree, Jonathan Richardson had used his knowledge to create the legal injunctions. Considered initially to be a left wing radical, he had slowly convinced the conservative government to his way of thinking. His successful civil litigations gained him notoriety and with press coverage many citizens had joined the cause. Negative comments about him had slowly fallen to the wayside. It was after his interview with the TBB National Network, his views became accepted and in line with the new movement. His group was on a path to save the ancient forests of British Columbia. Jonathan Richardson had used his university connection to gain the support of research scientists. The grants had allowed him to continue research on polymers. The invention of a material superior to wood was created. With the assistance of his scientific colleagues, he had created enviroplastics. The new product found its niche in the construction trade. Buildings constructed of these polycarbonates, were considered more cost effective than wood products.

The Panax Corporation had gone public some years prior and the shares on the Dow Jones Index had quickly risen. Enviroplastics had made its name in the construction industry. Architects, engineers and builders were hooked on this new substance as the building material of the future. Developers were quickly assured of the superiority of the polymers and welcomed them in the building trade. Environmentalists were now beginning to convince North American citizens the new technology would prevent the decimation of forests for coming generations. Jonathan Richardson LL.B. had proven his case and used enviroplastics as the solution to save the environment. He had been successful in his bid to improve the parkland. With the closure of each logging firm, he had pushed forward in his crusade. He persuaded many companies to pursue the improved technology, which would eventually save the environment.

The death of Dr. Jobin was the first time in the history of his firm, a member had been murdered. There had been many threats by fringe groups but they were quickly silenced with the threat of civil litigation. Dr. Jobin's death was the first brazen act against the Panax Corporation. This would certainly create pandemonium for the employees and the board members. Jonathan Richardson would have to assure every member of their safety. He would use Telenet conferencing to convey the message to his employees. The Panax Corporation would minimize their contact with the public for now. Someone had shown disdain toward the company by killing one of its members. Jonathan Richardson would insist on a quick investigation to bring the perpetrator to justice. He cleared his throat and addressed his bodyguard in the front seat of the limousine.

"George we aren't going to park in our usual spot. Would you drive into the underground parking lot next to our building! We need to take a few precautions. Dr. Jobin was murdered earlier today and we don't need any other fatalities," he said reflectively. His bodyguard immediately obeyed the command. He activated his turning signal and made a left turn into the underground parking lot. Jonathan Richardson watched carefully from the confines of the back seat. As the vehicle descended the ramp into the underground parking area, Jonathan Richardson glanced at the Panax Corporation building. A brown cargo van with a plumbing logo stamped on it, was parked in the loading zone in front of his office tower. Jonathan Richardson could see occupants in the front seat but was unaware of the camera inside the vehicle focused on his limousine as it made its way into the bowels of the underground parking lot.

George Blundel stopped at the gate and took the yellow receipt delivered by the automatic dispenser. He then proceeded slowly toward the parking zone for limousines. The extended black vehicle was backed slowly into the space and the keys in the ignition withdrawn. Jonathan Richardson waited patiently as his bodyguard left the front cab and then opened the door for him. The president of Panax Corporation glanced up at the man he had come to trust as his personal bodyguard.

"Don't worry about me. I've taken the usual precautions George. I've worn my protective vest. I wonder how many Panax members will be hurt before these lunatics are taken into custody."

His bodyguard did not say a thing but only listened carefully to his employer. He had been in the military for 25 years and had recently retired. He had seen action in the Mideast as a front line combat officer. In comparison to his military position, the trouble at Panax seemed mild. He would be wary and trust his instincts. Panax Corporation paid him a good salary to take care of its president. He motioned to Mr. Richardson to follow and led the way to the underground tunnel connecting the two buildings. They would enter the Panax building at the basement level, and then work their way to the floor which housed the administrative offices. George Blundel had been well trained in military tactics. He would follow the code which had been ingrained in him since his early years of service in the military. As he made his way into the tunnel, he scanned the area for assailants. The ex-military officer crept forward cautiously, inspecting every hidden crevice which could pose a threat.

Jonathan Richardson experienced a slight tension in his chest as he moved forward. His blood pulsed through his brain as he followed the bodyguard through the underground maze. They would soon enter the private elevator which would take them to his office. His bodyguard extracted the keys from his jacket and unlocked the door. Jonathan Richardson followed and waited nervously as George Blundel closed and locked the entry. With his thumb extended, Jonathan Richardson depressed the sensor which read the biometric code stamped into his thumbprint. The door opened and they entered the elevator. Unlike many of his contemporaries, Jonathan Richardson had positioned his office on the third floor. He knew from his past experience, being located in a Penthouse office made it difficult to vacate premises during crises. The impact of the World Trade Centre still lingered in his mind. He had lost some associates in the disaster and it was shortly after Ground Zero, he had relocated his company. He glanced at his security officer. Once more Jonathan Richardson pressed his thumbprint to the electronic scanner and then entered the four digit number. The company engineers had designed this as an added safety feature. A special code was needed to allow an occupant admittance to the floor, housing the administrative offices. The heavy metal door opened quietly. His personal secretary was standing at the entrance to greet him.

George Blundel excused himself and entered a room located near the elevator. He would spend his time in solitude, monitoring the security system which scanned the grounds in the vicinity of the Panax building. His new position was a welcome change to the action he had experienced in the combat zone. George Blundel would be ready in the event trouble arose. The aging military officer removed his Tufshield protective vest and sat at his desk. Two semi-automatic weapons were extracted from their leather holsters and placed them on the desk in front of himself. They would be in easy reach if he was called into action. With restricted access to Mr. Richardson's office, the only people allowed to enter were the administrative secretary and George Blundel. The office would remain a safe haven for its occupants. George Blundel activated the monitors and redirected the cameras to the hallways leading to the office floor. The video cameras located on each level of the Panax building would allow him to scan the interior and the exterior of the building. They were positioned in a location which secured them from the visible eye. The ex-military officer would be ready.

CHAPTER 2

The fiery red ball was rising from the east, casting its rays on the luminous structures. Huddled at the edge of the rooftop, Emerald Lee thought back to his days as a mercenary fighter in Iraq. The sweltering heat antagonised his body but couldn't diminish the exhilaration of the kill. Each squeeze of the trigger stimulated his adrenalin and fed his aggressive hunger. Killing under the guise of employment, had allowed Emerald Lee to act out the dark impulses which had driven him since adolescence. Fed by his memories, the impulses raged within. Once again, he would satisfy his darkest urges. He sensed the present draw upon him and the images from his past fade. He had been hired for this assignment, and it was time to begin.

A cool northerly wind penetrated the shooter's clothing, and with each shiver his spine contracted. His mind wandered back to his adolescence. Emerald Lee wondered why he hadn't experienced life the way others had? There were few he could call friends. As far as he knew, none of his relatives were still alive. In his daydreams, he had often returned to the neighbourhood where he had experienced the challenges of childhood. He remembered few positive memories from those early days. Only one person in particular came to mind, as he reflected on his past. Mrs. Pearce, the old lady who lived in the apartment below him on Seventh Street was the only one who had ever shown him any kindness. She was simple in her ways but Emerald Lee humoured her because she always gave him some of her baked cookies. Many had mocked her and referred to her as a demented old fool, the echoes of past laughter echoed in his ears penetrating the hidden labyrinths of his brain. He knew they probably laughed at him as well.

Emerald excelled in his grades in highschool and had made it out of his sordid neighbourhood. He had survived the early days and achieved success in the Specialized Technology Program in Upper State College. Others from his neighbourhood were not so fortunate and had succumbed to the illicit drugs which flowed through the conduits of this slum area of New York.

Reaching into his leather case, Emerald Lee withdrew his arsenal. He caressed his specially engineered Mauser 6.5 millimetre rifle as he reflected back to the combat action he had seen in Iraq. The weapon had served him well during his mercenary battles and had the killing power needed for this assignment. As he drifted to his past, he recalled the excitement as the bullets neatly ripped holes through the enemy soldiers. His mind would once again relive this experience. He recalled the images of his victims crumbling onto the hot desert sand as the projectiles made their targets.

A pigeon fluttered near the edge of the rooftop. Emerald Lee retrieved the 6.5 Mauser and sighted in the helpless grey bird. The Zeus scope with its high resolution magnified the bird's head, he squeezed the trigger. A bullet did not explode from the barrel but only an audible click resonated, the gun was empty. He wondered what kind of cruel bastard would shoot a pigeon anyway? During his adolescence he spent many hours on the rooftops studying and feeding pigeons. In those early days, the pigeons were his only solace from the violence of his drunkened stepfather. The torment he suffered in his home had not been accepted well by his neighbours. But rather than assist his family, they had distanced themselves because of feared reprisals. His stepfather had been known to inflict personal vengeance on any outsider who interfered with the family. As the violence escalated in his home, his peers would not allow him to cross the threshold of friendship. Emerald turned from them and spent most of his private time with the birds that flocked to the roof top of his apartment building.

Emerald's mind returned to the present as he prepared for the assignment. Two full clips lay beside him. He had been hired to do the job, but had never met his employer. His past military commander had always made the contact, and provided him with the dossier. He remembered the day of his recruitment. It was a week following his return from Iraq, Emerald had been contacted. The targets were thoroughly researched and the details provided to him by his commander. The assignments came sporadically but the payment was more than sufficient to support his lifestyle. Emerald Lee had made the trip to Toronto by himself and carried out his last assignment. Two hits in two days would be a record for him.

He reflected back to his last assignment. The target had been a scientist employed with the Panax Corporation. Emerald Lee never knew the reason for their elimination. He had been hired as the shooter and was not in business to pass judgement. This assignment was no different than the ones he had known in other countries. He found his niche as a marksmen on the State College shooting team and had merely taken his skill to the next level. Emerald Lee never experienced any guilt for the assignments because they hadn't paid him to experience emotion, only to squeeze the trigger.

He had studied Dr. Jobin's daily pattern from a distance. The doctor's demise came swiftly, he had not suffered in his last moment on earth. The projectile crashed through the thin glass pane of the kitchen window and connected with its target. Dr. Jobin had been sitting at the kitchen table reading his paper. In his last moment of existence, his target had been at peace with himself. It was more humane and better this way, much better than dying in a facility for the Infirm like his dear friend Mrs. Pearce.

Emerald Lee never had personal contact with his target prior to the hit. It minimized any chance of remorse for his actions. When Emerald Lee squeezed the trigger, there was never any cognitive dissonance created in his mind. His reason for killing was money and the hit merely a job which had to be done. Today, he would once again squeeze the trigger and once again would make the kill. Then, he would escape without detection.

Muffled sounds drifted upward toward him. Thirty-fourth Street was coming to life. The time was quickly approaching and the assassination would be carried out as planned. Gazing down at the street, he could see his target. Dr. Milano had just emerged from his black Mercedes 5000. Young school girls dressed in brightly coloured uniforms giggled as they strolled past the building complex. Memories from his past raced to the present. The lone sniper never had much success with adolescent relationships while he attended Luther Highschool. The girls in his class had always refused his advances and called him a low-classed moron. After a few negative encounters, he relinquished his interest in adolescence romance but had gained companionship from his frequent visits to Embassy Escort Service. In the last year, he met a waitress and now had an ongoing relationship.

Emerald Lee sighted in the businessman as he crossed the street toward the Panax Corporation building. Once again, his contractual work as a mercenary soldier would give his life some purpose. He focused the scope on his target as the businessman approached the front doors of the office building. His marksmen skills were once again being called into action. Ever so lightly his index finger slowly squeezed the trigger. The silencer on his rifle muted the sound of the exploding bullet. The high velocity projectile crashed forward making its impact. Dr. Milano crumbled to the concrete sidewalk. Two more shots echoed in quick succession at the downed man. His commander had taught him to always hit them at least twice after they went down. It would ensure the kill.

Surveying the scene below, he returned his rifle to its case. He did not see the special agent in the suit running toward the downed victim. He hadn't counted on anyone being in the vicinity. With his Glock automatic raised, the security officer scanned the rooftop. As his vision connected with the shooter, a staccato of quick shots were fired at the unknown assailant. Emerald Lee didn't have time to dodge the bullets. The metal projectiles sliced through the air and only the wisp of the wind was detected as the copper softpoints burrowed themselves into the shooter's body. Both shots had connected, one in his shoulder and the other in his lower abdomen. The wounded sniper knew he had to leave quickly or he wouldn't make it out of the combat zone. The tempo of the activity reached a heightened crescendo in the street below. Within minutes, a cruiser with sirens blaring screeched to a halt next to the security officer. Emerald Lee knew he had to leave immediately, but was unable to slip undetected from his position on the rooftop.

The rays of the rising sun filtered in from the east and slightly blinded his vision of the street below. He thought back to his last hit in Toronto. It had been easy, but this one was different. Two officers sprung from the front seats of their vehicle. With their weapons drawn, they scanned the rooftop for the shooter. Emerald Lee would have to hold his position, otherwise they would detect him. Within minutes, two more police cars stopped abruptly below. Weapons were aimed in the direction of the rooftop as the officers swarmed the building. He could not wait any longer, Emerald Lee would have to move fast if he wanted to get out. He'd already been pinned down for ten minutes. As he watched helplessly, a truck pulled up in front of the building. With his weapon retracted from its case, a volley of shots were fired from his rifle into the side of the vehicle. He watched the SWAT team dressed in black uniforms leap through the open rear door, dodging the randomly fired bullets. A loudspeaker crackled in the distance as the chief of operations fumbled with the switches.

"You're surrounded! Throw down your weapon!"

Emerald contemplated his predicament for a fleeting moment, then sent off another volley of projectiles into the street below hoping to create a diversion. The officers knew they were dealing with a madman, they had encountered his type before. The commander of the Tactical Unit bolted into the building. Other uniformed men dispersed according to plans. Emerald continued with his assault, shooting at shadows which moved below. He re-positioned himself behind a rooftop vent, bracing himself for the counter-attack.

The situation was familiar to one he had known from his past. His thoughts returned to the killing fields in Iraq. The enemy were quickly approaching and he was ready. They moved within twenty feet of him but did not detect his presence. He fired his weapon quickly with its silver points tearing crisp holes through them. Their bodies twitched and then they were gone. The image faded, Emerald Lee realized he was not in Iraq. Below, he could hear the fire escape creak under the weight of his pursuers. The rifle exploded twice as he sighted the men in uniform approaching the rooftop. The first shot ripped into the unknown man's face, jerking his body backwards. The next shot caught the second cop in the chest. Crawling toward the fire escape, Emerald did not see the door of the stairwell exit crash open. Guns were aimed in his direction. He did not react quickly enough to dodge the projectiles launched in his direction. The shots only became audible as a burning sensation seared into his right shoulder. The projectile ripped its way through his neck exploding his collarbone as it exited through the front of his shoulder. Emerald Lee lay motionless as footsteps on the rooftop cautiously approached him. His hand caressed the stock of the Mauser rifle as he attempted to roll onto his back to fire a round at his unknown assailant. Emerald Lee did not get the chance to fire another round but only experienced the ensuing blast from the handgun as two more bullets buried themselves deeply into his chest. The police officer had trusted his instinct and fired at the downed assailant.

Detective Lieutenant Brown gripped his Glock semi- automatic handgun. The barrel was still warm from the shots he had just fired. He inched his way slowly toward the assailant as his heart pounded from the excitement of the moment. With his gun still aimed at the sniper's head, he kicked aside the rifle. Blood was oozing from the sniper's wounds. He focused on the man's face expecting to see a hideous cretin. The face did not reveal the expected lunacy. He muttered at the insanity of the situation. A member of the Tactical Unit knelt down and checked his fellow officer's pulse and then shook his head. Detective Brown knelt beside the shooter his fingers sensing the wounded man's pulse. Blood still pumped through the sniper's jugular vein.

He muttered quietly the sniper was still alive. Detective Brown suppressed an irresistible urge to finish off the assailant. His mind drifted back to the desert in Saudi Arabia. When the enemy was down, you always completed the job. His commanding officer had always insisted a bullet through the temporal lobe was the added insurance. Detective Brown stared at the assailant. He retracted the barrel of his firearm from the side of the sniper's head and holstered the weapon. He could hear the ambulance in the distance howling as it approached the building. Within minutes, the medical vehicle arrived. He could hear the paramedics below, screaming orders and saw a body on the street strapped to the stretcher. A second team of paramedics reached the rooftop. They quickly moved from body to body inspecting each downed man. Detective Brown instructed them to take the downed sniper and then followed closely on their heels as the stretcher made its way to the street.

"I'll ride with this one to the hospital. I'm not letting this killer out of my sight," he muttered. Detective Brown climbed into the ambulance and stared out through the small rear window as the vehicle raced forward with its sirens screaming. People were once again milling cautiously on the streets. The only reminder of the morning's madness were the red stains on the concrete sidewalk. The blood would soon be washed into the sewers by the cleanup crew. He turned to watch the paramedic administer first aid to the assailant's wounds. The ambulance rocked in steady motion as it weaved its way through the morning traffic on Second Avenue. A verse stored in his distant memory aroused Detective Brown's thoughts. Was it Patton or Mills who had said it? He had used it once on a term paper in his criminology class. Detective Brown mumbled the words. "The man who regards his own life and that of his fellow creature as meaningless is hardly fit to live."

Detective Brown cursed as he contemplated the senseless slaughter. Once again he thought back to his impulse to finish the sniper as he lay dying. Detective Brown wasn't sure he had made the right decision when he holstered his handgun. His attention once again focused on the motionless assailant. Intravenous tubing allowed life to seep into the still body. He wondered why the sniper deserved any more humane treatment than he had shown the New York police officers? Detective Brown's method would give the sniper the same mercy he had shown his victims. Detective Brown fondled the weapon in his holster as he inspected the unconscious madman. He knew he would have to control his impulses. In his mind, Detective Brown knew this was the only difference between the madman and himself. The idea nagged at his conscience as he rode in silence starring at the unconscious sniper.

Tires screamed as the ambulance came to an abrupt stop. An odour of burning rubber permeated Brown's nostrils. Memories of suicide victims were retrieved from his past. These were the same smells he had come to experience when victims used shotguns to terminate their lives. A slight nauseous feeling overcame him. Attendants wheeled the sniper's body from the ambulance and darted for the emergency entrance. Detective Brown leaped out and stumbled as his feet hit the pavement. The attendants rushed past the nurses toward the emergency operating room. Detective Brown felt stifled by the mixed aromas of cleansing agents and the odour of death. Once inside the emergency room, the sniper was quickly examined by the attending physician. Detective Brown could vaguely hear the doctor's comments. The sniper was haemorrhaging internally and needed immediate surgery.

"Why don't you have a seat in the waiting room officer, this guy isn't going anywhere," muttered the physician.

Detective Brown stared at the nurse standing next to the physician. She reminded him of a waitress he once knew during his training on Paris Island. He experienced a brief fond memory, and then followed the nurse into the waiting area. The room was stark with its plastered white walls and ceiling. He sunk into a chair. Lieutenant Brown had been working on the Martinez murder and had spent most of the evening at the precinct pouring through the documents. The early morning call had taken him to the crime scene just at the time he should have been going home. Detective Brown was exhausted, he hadn't slept for 36 hours. A deep sleep quickly overtook him.

CHAPTER 3

"Detective Brown! Detective Brown!" a distant voice beckoned him. A hand pressed lightly on his shoulder rousing him from deep sleep. Brown peered through puffy eyelids, attempting to focus on the image.

"The guy you brought in this morning. He's pulled through surgery. It looks as though he's going to make it. I thought you'd like to know," said the nurse. Detective Brown focused on the large illuminated clock in the waiting room. It was ten o'clock. He had slept for almost 2 hours. The words reverberated through his mind. The sniper was going to recover. The officer wasn't sure whether he felt elated or depressed. Slowly, he rose from his seat and walked toward the nurse's station.

"Nurse, where can I find a phone?" he asked.

"Down the hall, first right," was her reply.

Exhausted, Detective Brown made his way through the maze. He noticed the phone suspended from the paint chipped wall. Lack of funds in the hospital had left little money for repairs. Placing his hand in the left trouser pocket he inched into the depths and his fingers caressed a hairy thigh. "Shit," he muttered. Searching his sports jacket, he withdrew a quarter and deposited it into the telephone coin receptacle. As he pressed the buttons, he realized once again his fingers were too large to properly dial the number.

"What kind of assholes do the telephone companies have working for them? They should take a few lessons in equipment design," he muttered.

"Precinct 14," a female voice answered.

"Give me homicide," he barked. Lieutenant Brown recognized the voice of the officer at the other end.

"Martinelli this is Lieutenant Brown. I'm at New York Hospital. The sniper is going to live. Send two officers down here right away. I want arrangements made to transfer the murderer to the Clinton Correctional Facility. I want round the clock surveillance until this guy is in confinement. I'm in the waiting area down the hall from recovery. I'll be here when they arrive. Let Captain Smith know what's going on. He's probably at the mayor's office right now trying to work something out. The press is going to have a field day with this one."

Detective Brown hung up the phone and returned to the waiting area. He approached the coffee machine and inserted some coins. There were a number of choices. Black, black with sugar, black with whitener. Black with whitener he thought to himself. Detective Brown smiled to himself, he wasn't about to start changing his physical appearance. He liked his pigmentation the way it was and was proud of his African-American ancestry.

Thirty minutes passed as he waited on the uncomfortable hospital chair. Several times he stood up and paced between the coffee machine and the waiting room. He was staring down at a crushed cigarette butt on the floor when he heard the familiar sound of leather heels. Looking up, he noticed two police officers approaching.

"Martinelli! What the hell are you doing here?"

"Why are you always giving me shit. I couldn't find anyone but Arsenault. Everyone is busier than hell. It wasn't my choice to come down and relieve you," replied the overweight cop. Detective Brown shook his head in disgust as he looked at Constable Martinelli. He wondered what was happening at the police academy? Why were they unable to recruit good men for the force? Bums like Martinelli lingered on at the precinct and gave the police department a bad image.

"Martinelli! Why can't you look a little more presentable? Tuck in your shirt! You look like a slob!" barked Detective Brown. Martinelli looked down at his protruding stomach and thought back with fondness to the supper his wife had prepared for him the night before. He quickly stuffed his spaghetti stained shirt back into his pants.

"I want this homicidal maniac transferred out to the Clinton Correctional Facility and there better not be any slip ups." Detective Brown frowned as he walked off. Some day he would be promoted to captain and then things would change at the precinct. The department standards were slipping and all types of undesirables were getting accepted into the force and ending up in his precinct. He wondered how the applicants were getting past the screening tests? The shrinks weren't doing their job, he thought to himself. They were spending too much time fraternizing with the captain and playing the political games. Everyone was looking out after their own interests and the precinct was suffering. Things would change when he was promoted.

He walked past the orderlies carrying supplies to the ward. The escape hatch at last, he thought to himself as he pushed open the large front doors. Detective Brown sucked in the cool morning air as he walked down the steps. He gestured with his hand to the waiting cab. The dented yellow taxi made a U turn and pulled up at the front steps. Detective Brown jumped into the cab and mumbled the address to the driver. The smell of alcohol and cheap perfume wafted up from the stained seat cushion. He rode in silence as the cab made its way through the interior of the city.

Detective Brown contemplated the lives of the undesirables who resided in New York. They were always creating problems for the citizens of the great city.

His dad had taught him to be an achiever. It had been the only way to make it out of his neighbourhood. Detective Brown had been successful and had gone the distance. His parents had offered him the money for a college education. They had made many sacrifices so he could break from the chains which weighed heavily on his shoulders. In the end, his African-American ancestry had motivated him to excel. His father's Baptist ideals had driven Detective Brown beyond the values of the street. He wasn't big on religion but he had obtained his moral values from the holy book and sometimes used them to make his decisions.

Fifteen minutes later, the cab was out of the smelly interior of the city. As it sped into the driveway of his apartment building, large droplets of water pelted the windshield. Detective Brown paid the driver and got out. He enjoyed the exhilarating sensation of the water splashing down on his face. Rain was good for the city of New York. It renewed the air and washed the filth and stench into the sewers. He often imagined forcing crime into the sewers in the same manner. He didn't think himself obsessed with his job, but knew without people like himself on the force, anarchy would soon prevail and override the city.

Detective Brown didn't have any close friends at the precinct. There wasn't any time for friendships and those who did talk to him, did so only out of respect, they owed it to him. He had kept the streets free of crime and made it safer for citizens. He entered the building and quickly walked up the flight of stairs to his apartment. His fingerprint was quickly scanned by the biometric reader, allowing him to enter the apartment. As he closed the door, Detective Brown felt a sense of comfort. It would temporarily shut out the madness of the city. The sanctity of his home would soon envelop him in a warm cocoon.

After pouring himself a glass of his favourite scotch, he reclined on the sofa. Music from the local jazz station filtered from his stereo system. Over the past week, a number of homicides had created havoc for the police department. The cases were piling up on his desk and they weren't being solved quickly enough. There was too much paper work and too many smart defense lawyers handling the cases. It was almost impossible to get a conviction unless you had an air tight case. Circumstantial evidence didn't cut it with the judges anymore. They wanted hard facts. The defense attorneys were eating up the prosecutors and there wasn't a thing Detective Brown could do about it. He had been told to terminate his strong armed tactics because the judges didn't accept the forced confessions anymore. Detective Brown knew the criminals had too many rights. He wondered about the rights of the victims? He questioned his reasons for becoming a cop? In his mind, he knew it was a tough way to make a living.

Detective Brown sank into the soft foam cushions as he contemplated his new case. This one would be different. The ballistic report would match up with the bullets removed from the officers' bodies. Those retrieved from the murdered businessman would be from the same rifle. The casings on the rooftop would be gathered by the Forensic unit. Other officers had witnessed the sniper shoot the police officers on the roof. Even if the defense lawyer argued lack of evidence in the murder of the downed businessman, there would be witnesses who had seen the police officers fall in combat. Detective Brown had been there when his partner took the projectile. He would be there to testify for the two officers who had died during battle.

Detective Brown sipped at the warm liquid. The alcohol would free his thoughts and relax his mind. He felt himself slipping into a trance like state. His mind fixed upon an earlier period in his life. Detective Brown had liked school but had lived for football. His coach had recognized his potential. He had been picked as the first string quarterback because of his agility. Winning had been his only drive during those early years. He still felt the same way about life as a cop, only his focus had changed. Detective Brown had been instrumental in his school's win of the Eastern championship. Purdue had offered him a football scholarship, but he decided on a career with the army. The glory of war had left its mark in his neighbourhood. His dad had fought in the Vietnam war and was treated as a hero when he returned to the city. His dad's reward was a prestigious government job. But later in life, his father had found his path as a Baptist minister. Detective Brown wanted to make a name for himself. Football had given him his first taste of recognition, but the army would guarantee greater rewards. There was stiff competition in football and it took too long to succeed. Besides, he liked the risks associated with war. It was similar to the win or lose situation he had known in football and satisfied his aggressive drive.

Detective Brown could feel himself slipping. His breathing slowed and his chest heaved slightly. His mind was drifting back to an earlier time. They were pinned down in a trench, bullets ripped overhead. The captain yelled at Corporal McFadden to get out of the trench and knock out the enemy guns. McFadden didn't react but stared into space. Sweat streamed down his face. Fear had caused him to piss himself. The captain withdrew his pistol and ordered McFadden out under the threat of having his brains blown out. The frightened soldier only trembled. Turning his head to the captain, Brown shouted McFadden had snapped. Brown volunteered to go instead. He knew they were finished anyway. He would rather take it in the chest than be run over by the enemy. A constricted sensation tore at his throat and blood surged through his cerebral arteries. He inhaled two deep breaths and sprang to the top of the trench, rolling as he hit the dirt. Football fans cheered as Brown sprinted down the field. With the speed of a jackal he darted for the end zone. The stadium was in an uproar. Brown was going all the way. With a leap, he threw himself over the line and hit the desert floor. Stunned, he edged forward and scanned the area for the Iraqi soldiers. Guns were still blazing on the battlefield. The offensive was directed at the trench where he'd been only minutes before. Brown wondered whether the enemy had seen him? He wondered whether they thought him mortally wounded when he went down? He had escaped momentarily from their surveillance. As he looked up from the cover, he spotted three soldiers ten yards off. Brown slithered and edged his way to his prey. His pigmentation would be to his advantage. He could see his enemy clearly now. Silently he released the safety on his M16 and sprung from his hiding place.

"Eat this," he screamed. Both soldiers turned, the closest to him took the direct spray. The second was knocked into the pit, their trap had worked against them. Reddened metal rods protruded from the soldier's body. Approaching cautiously, he glanced at the motionless forms. Brown knew he had seen three soldiers. Nervously, he looked for the remaining one. He'd heard of the tricks the enemy had used to sucker the Americans. He approached cautiously, not removing his eyes from the area of combat. The downed soldiers' bodies were riddled with bullets. But he knew, you could never tell whether they were dead. His captain had made a remark, the enemy were like reptiles, you could never quite kill them. A sudden rustling alerted him to the soldier rushing toward him. A bayonet was fixed at Brown's abdomen. Reflexively, Brown jerked his M16 in the assailant's direction and pulled at the trigger, the gun didn't fire. Swinging it downward, he blocked the bayonet. The force knocked the rifle from the enemy soldier's hand. The soldier lunged for his boot and withdrew a knife. Brown jumped into combative stance, ready for his attacker. With the expertise of a black belt trained in art of oriental combat, he delivered a round house kick deep into the oblique muscles of the soldier's right side. The knife slipped from the enemy soldier's hand as he crumbled to sand. A hundred killing techniques flashed through Brown's mind as he delivered the heel of his boot into the soldier's temple. The impact crushed in his opponent's skull.

Sweat steamed down Brown's face. He was breathing heavily from the encounter. Examining the M16, he realized the clip hadn't been positioned properly. Only the sounds of distant gun battle broke the silence of the hot desert air. Cautiously, Brown picked his way back to the trench. At any moment, he expected to see the enemy charge out at him. McFadden's body was pressed against the wall of the trench with a handgun tightly clenched in his fist. The trembling soldier was frozen in position. The commander was motionless. Brown could see thick clotted blood oozing from the hole in the back of the captain's head. The other soldiers had deserted. This too was a casualty of war. Those in charge had often been murdered by their own men. It was simple concluded Brown, the college boy had made the fatal error of pushing the soldier to his breaking point.

"McFadden, we're getting out of here. Give me your hand," said Brown. A trembling arm moved in Brown's direction. He could see the expressionless gaze. Slowly, Brown removed the .45 calibre handgun from McFadden's tightened grip and lifted the broken soldier from the trench.

Chopper's could be heard in the distance. Brown suddenly awoke from his dream. The drone of the propellers was getting louder. He pulled himself from the couch and made his way slowly to the window overlooking the city. He could see the flashing lights of the helicopter making its way toward the tall buildings. Another causality, Brown thought to himself. Glancing at his watch, Detective Brown realized he'd slept for six hours. He looked out from his window over the west side of Manhattan. In a low guttural voice he muttered.

"I wonder what the slime are doing today?"

Detective Brown left the living room and walked into the washroom. Disrobing himself quickly, he stepped into the shower. The warmth of the water trickled down his spine. It felt good to his stiff muscles. He would have to stop falling asleep on his couch. The soft cushions were not providing the support to his lower back. The shower would remove the staleness of sweat from his body. After ten minutes under the spraying water head, he walked from the stall. He moved slowly from the bathroom and made his way to his bedroom. Thumbing through the shirts hanging in the closet, he realized there weren't any white ones left. Detective Brown knew he would have to start taking his laundry to the cleaners on a regular basis or get himself a wife. He caught himself momentarily as he thought of the dilemma.

Marriage would certainly infringe on his solitary lifestyle, he decided quickly to visit the dry cleaners.

A brisk warm wind enveloped his body as he left the air conditioned apartment building. He could feel the warm damp air work its way down his spine. The injury from his war wound still plagued him on damp days. Summer was slowly edging its way into New York. It's hot humid weather would show no mercy for the next three months. Traces of garbage would mire the streets and the stench would emerge from the overflowing gutters. He would have to experience the odiferous waste each day as he made his way to work. The intense heat would magnify the rotting putrid substances. Smog would blanket the city and crime would surface along with the sewer rats. He'd made the call to City Taxi and his favourite cab driver was waiting as he approached the yellow vehicle.

"Bert take me to New York Hospital," he demanded.

"Yes sir, Detective Brown!" said the cabbie.

Brown slammed the door of the taxi and the vehicle sped off. Detective Brown liked the respect the cab driver showed him, not condescending like some of the rookies he worked with at the precinct. Detective Brown knew the cab driver well. Bert Laberre had mentioned he was a Cajun from New Orleans. He never pried into Brown's affairs unless information was offered. In the working class neighbourhood where he had been raised, everyone minded their business. It was a rule, unless you had something to say you kept your mouth shut. Gossip wasn't tolerated and Brown wasn't big on people who talked of others when they were absent.

"That was some shoot out! I'm sure glad you weren't hurt. They said you emptied your magazine into that sniper. Tabernak what is happening to this city. It makes me want to pack up and move back to New Orleans," said Bert.

"Don't believe everything you hear Bert. I only put three slugs into that miscreant. The media are always looking for hype to sell their story. Those people don't know the meaning of a real job.

They make up a story and confabulate it with lies. If there was a law, I'd have them all locked up for sensationalism," said Detective Brown. Bert Laberre smiled as he glanced sideways to look back at his fare. The frenchman's greased back hair and pointed features reflected a rat like profile. He continued his nattering about the theories plying the airwaves. Detective Brown didn't comment. The drone of the cabbie's voice was like listening to his mother boring him to sleep with her endless stream of drivel. He tried to listen but found himself sinking into a trance like state. The car suddenly came to a sudden stop and Detective Brown's upper body jerked forward.

"We're here Detective Brown," said Bert.

The officer extracted a neatly folded twenty dollar bill from his wallet. He reached across the seat and handed the cabbie the money. He told Bert to keep the change. Verbal gratitude rang in Detective Brown's ears as he opened the door and stepped into the humid air. Bounding up the hospital stairs, he thought back to the football workouts at Queen's High. Conscious of the weight on his midline, he sucked in his stomach. He had gained thirty pounds since his football days. There was little time for workouts in the precinct gym. He just couldn't squeeze in the time any more. Crime had been on the rise and he was paid to do something about it.

The rookie was standing near the door of the emergency recovery room when Detective Brown arrived. He inquired whether Martinelli was inside with the injured sniper. The rookie shrugged his shoulders and pointed at the area near the nurse's station. Detective Brown hastily marched down the hallway. He could see Martinelli relaxing on the sofa with his feet propped up on a chair.

"Martinelli, why the hell are you sleeping on the job?" asked Detective Brown. Constable Martinelli snapped to attention. He had been dreaming up excuses in case Brown surprised him.

"I was just thinking! I mean I had a soar leg," quipped the overweight cop.

"Forget the excuses! Just do your job. Now what are the arrangements on the transfer for the prisoner?" he asked.

"I talked to the emergency room doctor and he said we couldn't move the prisoner. It could cause medical complications and he might die in the transfer," said Martinelli.

"Are you for real Martinelli? That maniac killed three people and you're worried about him dying in the transfer to the prison hospital. Get on the phone right now and make the arrangements. I want an ambulance and a medical team here in 30 minutes. I want this guy delivered to the Clinton Correctional Facility and I want two more officers down here to assist," demanded Brown.

Constable Martinelli wasn't waiting around to get further instructions, he knew from the tone of Brown's voice, he meant business. He had been in confrontation with his superior officer on a previous occasion and it had almost cost him his job. The overweight cop scurried off into the hallway. He counted his blessings because Lieutenant Brown usually came down harder. Gossip had spread through the precinct, Lieutenant Brown was next in line when the captain retired. Constable Martinelli did not want to get on Brown's bad side. Anyone who crossed Lieutenant Brown, would probably end up doing the beat on the streets of New York. The captain favoured Lieutenant Brown because he had more convictions than any other cop in Precinct 14. The criminals who tried to take advantage of him, usually ended up in the morgue.

Detective Brown walked back to the recovery room. He looked in through the small round window on the door. The sniper was lying motionless on the bed. He studied the injured man's profile. A three inch scar ran from the sniper's left eye downward to his cheekbone.

Detective Brown wondered whether an APIC would provide the information about the assailant's background? He had a hundred questions but knew the appointed defense lawyer would probably block most of them.

Detective Brown assumed a trance like state as he reflected on the past events. In the Iraqi dessert, they had their methods of extracting information from the captured soldiers. Brown knew one hour alone with the assailant would provide him with answers. The criminal justice system had changed since his early days on the force. The lawyers used their legal savvy to tie up the whole system. In Detective Brown's books it all boiled down to money. The longer the lawyers stalled the system, the more money they made. It didn't require much intelligence to realize scheming was going on in the criminal justice system. He knew all they had to do was clock up the hours and get reimbursement. It all boiled down to billable hours. Thirty minutes passed as Detective Brown examined the unconscious sniper through the portal of the door. Two cops approached Brown as he looked in through the window. He motioned them to follow him to the seating area.

"I don't think I've met you fellows?" said Brown.

Both officers quickly produced their shields. The tall Puerto Rican stepped forward.

"My name is Garcia and this is Gruber. We're new at Precinct 14. Only started about a month ago," he said proudly.

"The prisoner doesn't appear to be going anywhere. He's just been through major surgery. They extracted five bullets. Its a shame we didn't finish the job. Watch him, regardless of his condition. His legs are shackled to the bed. Keep the blankets over him. I don't want anyone leaking information to the press we are mistreating the prisoner. You know how those dimwits from the press like to make a big thing out of nothing. I hope you guys can do a better job guarding the prisoner than Martinelli," said Brown. The two rookies looked at one another and burst into laughter. They knew Martinelli well. He had become a joke at Precinct 14. Detective Brown walked briskly as he left the hospital. He had to complete some paper work, if he was going to get the transfer done correctly. He would follow the rules, he didn't want anything getting out to the assailant's lawyer. Forensics had worked quickly on this case. They had already been in contact with the Toronto Metro Police Service. According to the report, the assailant was a suspect in the Jobin murder. From the information he had received, Detective Brown knew this was probably the same sniper who had killed the Panax executive. He would be talking to the Canadian police and comparing the modus operandus. According to the classified data, ballistics had identified the weapon. Detective Brown smiled as he thought of the sniper in custody. He would make sure the assassin went down for his crimes.

CHAPTER 4

Two slender figures moved slowly along the wet concrete sidewalk. The muggy evening air encompassed their lightly clad bodies. A light breeze from the south cooled the perspiration which had forced its way to the surface of their clammy skin. Neon lights glittered in the distance.

"Its awfully muggy for this time of year! The weathermen have been talking about global warming. What do you think?" asked Jilian.

"Why don't we take a short cut across the park. I know of a quaint little bar where we could get a beer and cool down before we go home," said the tall brunette.

"Sounds like a good idea to me, but I don't think we should take a short cut through the park. You know what the newspaper has been saying about the Park Rapist," said Jilian.

"Jilian most of those incidents happened in North York and Scarborough. This is downtown Toronto and there haven't been any reports of the Toronto rapist in this area," said Anne.

"Okay but let's make it quick. I don't feel safe walking through the park at night. Besides the darkness always gives me the creeps," responded Jilian. The two friends quickened their pace. They glanced nervously from side to side as they hurried along the muddy pathway. Only the water slopping on their soles broke the silence of the night. Anne could hear the belaboured breathing of her companion. She could sense her heart beating quickly as she maintained the pace.

"I don't think we should have come this way Anne, my feet are almost soaked," said the tall blonde.

"I think you're right! Let's turn back. I guess it wasn't such a bright idea. It would have taken us more time the other way, but at least our feet wouldn't be soaked. I'll probably have a cold by tomorrow," said her friend. As the two women turned to retrace their steps, a figure loomed in the distance.

"Holy shit! Do you think that guy has been following us?" blurted Anne.

"Hey you! You had better get your ass out of here. Our boyfriends' are just behind us," yelled Jilian brazenly. The figure suddenly disappeared into the foggy night. Echoing footsteps of the fleeing intruder were now barely audible.

"You have to know how to deal with these assholes Anne. Remember this isn't New York. When someone tries to get the vantage point, you have to challenge them. They will usually back down. If that doesn't work, I have a nice little treat for their eyes." Jilian withdrew a small can of mace from her leather shoulder bag and showed it to her anxious friend. Anne held the can, her eyes straining as she studied the label. She was convinced that Jilian was a survivor. Her friend always had an answer even in the worst of times. Anne had been taking assertiveness training courses and was determined to develop the self-confidence her friend possessed. Anne moved closer to her friend. She could sense the moistness of her friend's arm brush lightly against hers. Both women quickened the pace toward the street light in the distance. The leaves lightly rustled on the trees as the wind blew intermittent gusts. The breeze seemed cooler to Anne's bare skin now. She wondered whether the temperature was actually dropping or whether primal fear was working its way into her spine. She heard a branch snap in close proximity. The hair on Anne's bare arms stood on end as she cautiously glanced in the direction of the noise.

"What the hell was that Jilian?" she asked.

"It was probably a branch falling from a tree. Look how windy it has gotten," responded her friend.

"No it wasn't a branch falling. I'm sure it came from the bushes over there," said Anne pointing a finger in the direction.

"Let's get out of here before we spook ourselves," responded Jilian.

The street light was now only a matter of metres away but to Anne it seemed like a mile. The quicker she walked, the further their destination seemed. Images of violence flashed through her mind. Only two years ago, she had been chased on the university campus. If it hadn't been for the patrolman, she would certainly have been attacked. As the thought rose from its depths, she tried to repress it. The trauma of the past experience still lingered and left a nauseous feeling in her gut. She tossed back her head determined to reach the safety of the street light. The brightly lit sidewalk ahead would provide her with sanctuary from the deep seated fear of her past. Only the beat of her heart and the noisy water dripping from her soles echoed as the young woman neared the edge of the park.

Without warning her friend was snatched from her side. Muffled sounds broke from Jilian's lips. Anne could only hear whimpers as Jilian fought with her captor. Anne froze in terror. She could see the attacker ripping the blouse from her friend's body. Anne's mouth opened widely but she could not scream for help. The words would not leave her lips. Only the crying and struggling of her friend were audible to the overwhelming sense of panic which encompassed Anne's brain. Anguished words worked their way from Jilian's vocal cords breaking the silence of the night. Anne could hear her name. She snapped out of her state of panic and dashed frantically toward the illuminated sidewalk. Branches pelted her face as she bolted through the shrubs blocking her escape route. Welts from the stinging projectiles were washed with the tears and sweat which trickled down her face.

"Help! Help us!" screamed Anne as she ran into the path of the oncoming cars. Vehicles swerved to avoid the hysterical female. Pedestrians hurried their pace, afraid the young desperate female was drug crazed and dangerous. Bystander apathy had once again risen as a byproduct of the violent society which Anne embraced. Citizens fearing for their lives, did not want involvement in another person's tragedy. Fear of personal violence created a sense of panic and they quickly moved away from the screaming woman. Frantically, Anne ran along the street in search of aid. In the distance, the neon lights swirled above the building. The pizza shop was now steps away. She crashed through the door, hysterically pleading with the attendant for assistance.

"My friend! My friend! She's being attacked in the park," screamed Anne. The young Italian pizza maker nervously looked at his friend and then leaped over the countertop.

"You call the cops Luigi! Tell them to get their asses down here quickly. Looks like we've got another rape going down. Show me where she is! Hurry before it's too late!" blurted the muscular attendant wearing the sleeveless undershirt and a stained white apron.

"I can't go back there! He'll kill me! He'll kill me!" she cried hysterically. Anne froze in her steps. She refused to budge from the safety of the Pizza shop. In desperation, the young Italian raised his hand and slapped her. Anne snapped from the hysteria and followed the pizza maker from the store.

"Over there! Over there!" she uttered helplessly.

Luigi Tamini had dialled 911 and the telephone dispatcher alerted to the emergency. The police had been contacted and were on their way. Two rookie police constables looked at one another disappointedly as they glanced down at their steaming hamburgers. It always seemed the calls came pouring in just when they were about to eat. They shoved their meal back into a brown bag and rose from the table. Entering their police cruiser, one of the young cops activated the emergency lights. The cruiser sped toward the location the dispatcher had given them. With the lights flashing, the car accelerated along Yonge Street in the direction of the reported crime.

"What do you make of it Jim? I'd like to get rid of those bastards! They're not only terrorizing women in this city, but also spoiling my supper," he stated. Bob Strang glanced at his partner and smiled. Both rookies had been with the Metro Police Service for six months and had seen their share of crimes. This was going to be different, neither had been called to a rape scene. Tension caused Constable Strang to chew at the inside corner of his mouth. He steered the vehicle toward the park. Moisture collected on the palms of his hands as he tightly clutched the steering wheel.

"This is Badge 57 calling dispatcher. We're heading for High Park. We'd like some back-up," said the tense constable. He depressed the accelerator. Bob Strang wanted to make it to the scene before other officers arrived. If he and his partner could take down the assailant, it could get them a commendation. It would be useful for a later promotion.

Detective Sergeant James was in the vicinity when the call came in. The plain clothes homicide detective fumbled with the radio in his unmarked car.

"This is Sergeant James calling. I'm at the intersection of Yonge and Gerard. I'm heading for High Park." He depressed the gas pedal and his vehicle accelerated. The stake out at the Panax building hadn't given up any clues. The drive to the park would not take him long and then he would return to the Panax building.

The young Italian grabbed Anne by the shoulder as he lead her into the park.

"Now show me where she was," he shouted.

"Over there! In that direction," she blurted.

"You had better stay here and direct the cops when they show up. I'm going to look for your friend," he shouted. Dropping his stained apron to the sidewalk, he ran into the cover of the bushes and disappeared. Anne sunk to the sidewalk in fear. She hadn't been able to recover her senses. Her heart still beat wildly and she sobbed hysterically. The Italian pizza worker struggled through the foliage. He hadn't been in the country long and wondered why he always found himself involved in other people's affairs. He cautiously glanced from side to side as he scanned the area for the assailant and the victim. He stepped forward and noticed the torn blouse crumpled beside the tree. His heart beat rapidly and he sensed a dryness in his mouth. He gulped quietly but couldn't swallow because of the lack of saliva. He bent over and retrieved the torn blouse. An aromatic fragrance wafted to his nostrils as he held it closely to his face. His pupils dilated as he scanned the area once more for the assailant. A faint rustling caught his attention. As he neared the dense undercover, he could see a pair of torn slacks thrown on the grass. Muffled sounds were now audible off to his left. He moved carefully toward the area and noticed the large man retracting himself from the naked woman.

"What the hell are you doing?" The young pizza worker blurted out in fear.

The half-crazed rapist swung quickly and withdrew a shiny object from his boot. Cautiously, the young Italian moved toward the assailant and delivered a kick, deep into the rapist's abdominal cavity. As the assailant staggered to regain his balance, the young pizza worker moved in for the offensive. Quickly recovering from the blow to his abdomen, the rapist slashed at the young Italian, cutting deeply into his left thigh. An anguished cry pierced the stillness of the park. The pizza worker did not regain his position quickly enough to avoid the rapist's oncoming foot to his head. He sunk into unconsciousness as his body crumpled onto the grass.

Anne did not see the patrol car pull up to the curb behind her. She had been mesmerized by the yell which had broken the silence.

"Where is he?" yelled the husky officer. Anne could only point. The two constables instantaneously withdrew automatic weapons from their holsters and moved into the darkness. The lead officer held his flashlight to illuminate the area. In the distance, they could hear the moaning of a female. Constable Strang was the first to see the assailant hovering over the naked woman.

"We've got you covered! Hands up and turn slowly! Cuff him Bob," he yelled to his partner. The surprised rapist turned quickly. He could see the officers moving in on him. Grabbing his victim, he pulled her naked body in front of him.

"You boys had better back off or I'm going to cut her," the rapist barked as he held his knife menacingly to the young woman's throat.

"Back off or the broad gets it! Now drop your guns!" shouted the rapist. The accent was familiar to Constable Strang. He had heard the same dialect used in his home town on the east coast. Slowly, the confused rookies backed away. Their guns still pointed at the rapist's head. The rookies glanced at one another. They had been taught at the Police Academy never to surrender weapons to the enemy. Now, they were faced with a hostage dilemma.

"You heard me you bastards! Do it or I cut her," shouted the half-crazed assailant. A guttural whine emerged from the naked helpless victim. Constable Blackburn slowly lowered his gun and let it drop to the muddy soil. He looked at his partner.

"Bob get rid of it! He'll kill her! He means it!" muttered the frightened cop.

"This won't go over big with our captain," said the other constable.

"This is different! Can't you see our predicament? If we don't surrender our weapons, he is going to slash her throat," said the frightened rookie.

"What about us?" shouted Constable Strang. He hesitated momentarily and then let his gun slip to the damp ground.

"Now you boys move back from your guns and no stupid moves or she gets it," yelled the assailant. The rapist moved forward with the limp victim dangling from his arm. The knife still pressed to her throat.

"Now kneel!" shouted the rapist. The two rookies slowly sunk to the muddy earth. Bob Strang could feel the wetness seep in at his knees as his body compressed into the soil. The rapist quickly retrieved the guns.

"You cops think you're pretty sharp, eh? What else did they teach you in the Academy. Maybe you boys follow the rules too closely. Now look at the predicament you're in. Don't worry, I'm not going to kill you. What do you think I am anyway? I was just looking for a little action and you guys had to come along and spoil it. What's up with you anyway. I was just having a little fun. Besides this broad was asking for it," he laughed. The rapist walked over to Constable Strang. The young rookie did not see the boot in time, it connected with the officer's right side of his head.

"Well, that is what I think of your Academy rules hotshot," shouted the rapist.

Constable Blackburn moved quickly from his kneeling position. He wondered whether he could get to the attacker in time. The rapist quickly turned and the officer froze as he saw the gun aimed at his head. A loud explosion echoed breaking the silence of the park. Two more shots were fired in quick succession. Constable Blackburn tensed up, he did not sense the assailant's bullets ripping through his body. Glancing upward, he could see the rapist staggering backward. Time slowed in his panic strickened mind. The image reminded him of a football quarterback crumbling onto the turf. The rapist rested on his knees, as he strained to get a look at the man who had shot him. He attempted to raise his gun. One more shot was fired at point blank, the rapist collapsed onto the grass. His legs twitched twice and then were still. Bullets had ripped through his upper torso and the last one had hit him squarely in the forehead.

The trembling police officer strained through the moistness of his eyes to get a look at the approaching figure. The man walked over to the downed corpse and kicked the gun out of the rapist's hand. The constable recognized Sergeant James.

"What the hell happened here Blackburn? How did that asshole get your gun?" asked the cop. Sergeant James holstered his 7 millimetre handgun and walked over to the nude woman sobbing hysterically on the grass. He removed his suit jacket and draped it over her shoulders. The officer caressed the victim's hair and mentioned everything would be okay. He told her the rapist was dead. He glanced over at the uniformed officer and told him to get back to his car and call for assistance. They would need three ambulances and a hearst. He walked over to the downed pizza worker and ripped at the mans's pants. He used the frayed material to make a tourniquet. He applied pressure to the man's wound and made a knot with the cloth. Sergeant James walked over to the unconscious rookie. The officer was still breathing but would need immediate attention for the concussion. Sergeant James walked slowly over to the downed rapist and in a low voice mumbled something about getting a clear shot at the rapist's testicals. He glanced back at the uninjured rookie.

"Blackburn I thought I told you to get back to your car and radio for assistance. What the hell is taking you so long? Get moving," barked Sergeant James. Constable Blackburn snapped out of his stupor and made his way back to the cruiser. As he approached the lighted street, he glanced at the woman crouched in a fetal position sitting on the grass next to the curb. She did not say anything but rocked herself like a frightened child. The officer opened the car door and grabbed at the radio on the front dash.

"This is Constable Blackburn calling. Officer down! We have one hell of a mess over here in High Park! Send ambulances quickly!" he shouted. His anxiety had led to confusion. He did not remember everything Sergeant James' had said. Constable Blackburn approached the young woman crouched in a fetal position on the curbside.

"Your friend is going to be okay. She's alive. We've got everything under control," said the cop. The woman did not respond but only hummed a child's nursery rhyme. She stared blankly at the officer as he tried to console her. The tragedy had left its impact on the terror stricken woman. Constable Blackburn assisted the woman to her feet and walked her toward the police cruiser. He opened the rear door and sat the confused woman on the back seat then retreated to the crime scene.

"Sergeant James, the ambulances are on the way. They should be here shortly," he responded. The young rookie walked to his unconscious partner. He inspected his friend's jaw.

"Don't worry about him, he'll survive, it's only broken," said Detective James.

"How's the kid? If it weren't for him, the rapist might have gotten away. He deserves a medal for bravery," said Blackburn.

"Are you for real Blackburn? We've got one stiff, an unconscious cop, a raped woman and a kid who's bleeding to death and you're talking about medals. Get your head together Blackburn!" said Detective James.

Sirens screamed in the distance. Tires squealed to an abrupt stop near the cruiser. Constable Blackburn ran out to meet the attendants. Sergeant James could hear Blackburn shouting the orders. The ambulance crews hurried into the park and strapped the victims to the stretchers. Two attendants ran over to the rapist and lifted his body onto a stretcher.

"Get that bastard off the stretcher! The boy needs attention," shouted Detective James. The ambulance attendants tilted the stretcher and threw the corpse back onto the grass. Sergeant James waited in the stillness of the park. He fixed the light on the rapist's body. The men from forensics would soon be there to take the photographs. Sergeant James knew Internal Affairs would be on his back again. This was the fifth criminal he had killed in just over six months. In his mind, he knew his kills were justified. His fellow officers would have been murdered if he had not acted. He removed a package of cigarillos from his pocket and inserted the thin cigar between his mouth. Then, he walked back to his vehicle. Opening the car door, he slumped to the edge of his seat with his feet braced against the curbside. He glanced toward Blackburn's cruiser and stared at the woman rocking in the back seat of the vehicle. Lighting up the cigar, he chewed on the wine tipped end. Detective James thought back to the last homicidal maniac he had killed. The Toronto press had a field day with it. The rehabilitation groups had come down heavily on the Metro police department. Once more, there would be a hundred questions to answer. All types of reports would have to be filed. Sergeant James smiled as he inhaled the cigar dangling from his lips.

CHAPTER 5

Jonathan Richardson sat in his office overlooking the twinkling city lights reflecting upward from the street. It was early morning, he had just been contacted by his associates in New York. Tom Milano had been murdered. The police in New York city had the killer in custody. The president of Panax was beginning to breathe easier knowing the criminal was behind bars. But somewhere in the back of his mind, he wondered whether this was just the tip of the conspiracy. His thoughts reflected back to his farm in Orangeville. He wanted to return to the countryside, but his instincts told him he should remain in Toronto. Two of his associates had been murdered and he could be next on the list. He didn't think it a good idea leaving the sanctuary of his office. The assailants probably had him under surveillance. Jonathan Richardson reflected on his past when there had only been threats. Now his life had taken a different path. It would be just a matter of time before the assailants came looking for him. There hadn't been any demands yet, but he was sure they would come. Terrorists typically made an attack and then the demands followed.

Jonathan Richardson had notified Dr. Jobin's wife in Florida. It would be more difficult for him when he made the telephone call to New York. His younger sister had been married to Dr. Milano, she would have a difficult time coping with her husband's death.

Jonathan Richardson reflected on the coincidence of events. A hit list had been drawn up by some terrorist group and the names of his associates from Panax Corporation were on that list.

From the conversation with the police chief he learned the criminal investigators were still attempting to piece the information together. They had the modus operandus but they still needed a motive for the crimes. The Panax Corporation was in competition with other firms but Jonathan Richardson didn't think his opponents would resort to murder to get the vantage point. He realized there was no safe haven. When someone held a grudge anything could happen. This was not the first time a corporation had been threatened. At one time any company north of the 49th Parallel was a safe haven. Things had changed in the last decade, Toronto was no longer a safe refuge. He thought over the alternatives. He could return to his native city of Vancouver but the assassins would come looking for him. These were trained killers, they would find him. He needed a strategy and a vantage point. His father had a small cabin in northern British Columbia. He had visited the remote location during his youth. The camp located near Williams Lake could provide him with some cover and time.

Jonathan Richardson glanced at the furniture in his office as he sat at the control seat. He activated his Delano 5000 personal computer and typed in the information. The times of the departing flights were listed. He thought for a moment, but then hesitated before shutting down the screen. The phone rang, he listened intently to the caller, then hung up. He walked toward the open doorway and could see George Blundel inspecting the images on the monitor.

"George I was just talking with a detective at the Toronto Police Services. They have Dr. Milano's killer in custody, but have reason to believe the assassins will come for me. I think we should leave town." Jonathan Richardson left the room. He entered his office and sat on the leather sofa. With the television converter in hand, he activated the monitor. The talk show host was interviewing a movie celebrity. Jonathan Richardson stared intently at the screen, but the information did not register in his brain.

George Blundel had been sitting at the control panel most of the night. He had experienced his share of trouble. After leaving the military, he had worked with the Canadian Security Services. The CSS had been formed to work in conjunction with the military on foreign security measures. The ex-military officer studied the surveillance cameras. They had been placed strategically throughout the Panax Corporation property. A camera mounted in the underground parking lot showed two derelict figures sitting near the exit door. He watched as they passed a brown bag between themselves. It wasn't the first time, he had seen indigents bunking out in the heated underground parking lot. He thought it a little odd, because it was June and most of the winos had relocated to the parks. He wondered how the miscreants had made it past security.

George Blundel activated the monitor as he studied the two men on the screen. Cameras had been installed for visual contact but this was one of the times he would have liked audio to eavesdrop on the conversation. He focused the camera on the indigents and zoomed in on them. Their faces were clearer now. As he studied them, one man seemed familiar. The camera was now in focus and the picture relayed back to his monitor. He enlarged the photograph of the man. The face still did not register. He quickly sent the picture into the hard drive of his Delano computer and scanned them against the CPIC file. Pictures flashed in succession as the comparison was made. One of the pictures was a good match, it resonated repeatedly on the screen. A central computer bank at the Ottawa Forensic Investigative Branch was accessed for identification purposes. He activated the file and loaded it into a memory bank. A picture with aliases, flashed on the screen.

George Blundel thought back to his days in the military, as he focused on the man's face. He studied the picture and depressed a key which printed out a hard copy. With the images still on the screen, he moved to the next phase of identification. A button was pressed and the computer activated. Composites of known criminals stored in the central bank were compared with the photograph. He waited as the computer started it's search. He returned once more to the camera, which scanned the underground parking area. The two men were moving forward now into the passageway which led to the elevator at the lower level. Both men were carrying duffle bags strapped to their shoulders. As he watched their movements, his second computer monitor flashed the face of a known criminal offender on his screen. George Blundel studied the information sheet. The man had served time in federal penitentiary and was a citizen of the United States. He was listed as dangerous and had a past connection with the American Liberation Order, a paramilitary terrorist group. The security officer glanced back at the computer monitor. He saw one of the terrorists take a device from his duffle bag and attach it to the thumb print identification reader. George Blundel watched in astonishment as the elevator door opened. He would have to act fast. A telephone call was electronically sent to the Metro police department warning them of the situation at the Panax Corporation. It would be a matter of minutes before the Tactical Squad was notified and the team dispatched to the building. He depressed a second button, an alarm would notify Jonathan Richardson. George Blundel hurried past the computer terminal and unlocked a door. Two automatic weapons were taken from their resting place. Jonathan Richardson was jolted from his sleep by the alarm. He ran into the adjoining room.

"What is it George?" he asked nervously. George Blundel pointed to the monitor. Jonathan Richardson could see the two men in the elevator.

"When they reach the sixth floor they are in for a surprise. I've already activated the program, the metal doors will confine them. At least we have the benefit of surprise. Put on this Tufshield vest and helmet, we're going down the staircase. There may be others waiting for us. We'll make our way to the Security Room, and then wait until the police arrive. I'm hoping we can reach the room without confrontation," he added. George Blundel studied the camera monitor near the entrance. He watched the confused expression on the terrorist's faces as they looked at one another. One of the intruders withdrew an electronic device and positioned it over the display panel. He activated a switch but the door to the main building would not open. George Blundel had set the program in motion, the assailants would not be able to return to the lower floor by the elevator. They would not have access to the parking lot. We're going down the north face staircase. Here is the automatic weapon that I trained you to use. It's ready to fire."

George Blundel motioned to his boss to follow him. As he left the office, he activated a button to seal the office door. A timer would activate the explosive device, the blast would kill anyone within twenty feet of the office. Within minutes they were at the basement level. He cautiously opened the door. Jonathan Richardson followed as they made their way into the tunnel connecting the office building to the Security Room. The light on the ceiling of the parking garage flickered briefly as a slight tremor shook the building.

"I don't think we'll have to worry about them anymore. They shouldn't be a threat any longer. The police should be here soon and they can sort out the mess. You will have to replace the paint in the hallway", said George Blundel as he smiled.

"Is it legal to use that stuff?" asked Jonathan Richardson nervously.

"What stuff! It must have been something they were carrying. They were terrorists, weren't they?" said George Blundel. Both men made their way to Security room. Jonathan Richardson opened the door and was quickly followed by George Blundel. From their seats at the monitor they scanned the area using the strategically placed cameras.

CHAPTER 6

"This is Hank Bates with the 8:00 a.m. news. Here are some of the headlines for this morning. The Dow Jones Stock market has fallen three hundred points; a city detective guns down a rapist; and an explosion this morning at the Panax Corporation killed two men; now for the details."

Detective James could hear the drone of the radio from the bedside table as he lifted his weary body from the cotton bedsheets. From the warm sheets, he laboriously dragged his legs onto the wooden floor. Turning off the monotonic drone of the radio, he glanced at the clock which rested on the top of his dresser. He rubbed at his eyes so he could focus on the clock.

"I've overslept! I knew I should have returned to the Panax Corporation last night. I might have gotten in on some of the action. The chief is really going to chew me out on this one. I told those guys in surveillance to keep an eye on the building and give me a call if they saw something. If I hadn't left when I did, who knows what would have happened to Blackburn and his partner. And those stupid kids what were they thinking, walking through the park with a rapist on the prowl. I'd better get down to the gym for a workout before I go to the precinct, because shit is going to fly this morning. My facts had better be straight. I wonder if Tod will still be waiting when I get to the gym?" he asked himself.

Detective James lunged for the telephone and dialled the club number. With each ring he was getting more annoyed. Finally, he heard an audible click.

"Bloor Athletic Club, Jan Neuman speaking."

"Jan, this is Frank James. Have you seen Tod Miller this morning?" he asked.

"He's in the gym exercising," was her reply.

"Do me a favour and tell him that I'm going to be fifteen minutes late. Thanks I appreciate it," he said. He slammed down the receiver and slipped into his shorts and a cotton sweat shirt. With his business suit thrown into his duffle bag, he moved quickly from the apartment and down the set of stairs. He sprinted to his vehicle and unlocked the door of his Camaro. Inserting the key into the ignition, the 350 engine hummed as he pumped the gas pedal. Checking the rear view mirror, he backed his vehicle from its position and manouvered from the lot. This was the second time he was late in the past week. He knew his friend would be irritated. He wondered whether Tod would start the jog without him.

Over the past month, Detective James had noted some changes in his friend's behaviour. Many of his fellow officers had succumbed to the pressure of the job but he couldn't understand why his friend had been so edgy. Firefighters had a tense job, but didn't always have to explain their actions. Even though he did his job well, the Special Investigation Unit always wanted an explanation. He had saved the lives of two officers, a pizza worker and a university student but they would still want an explanation about the rapist. There wouldn't be any room for inconsistencies and only the facts of the case would matter. He would have to explain the reason for his departure from surveillance at the Panax Corporation. A lot of pressure would come his way. There was just too much paper work and not enough time left in the day to do his job properly. He thought about his friend Tod. He never had to do any explaining. Firefighters, only had to file a report on the incident, the cause of the blaze, and the rest was up to the firemarshal. No one questioned their motives or rarely gave them a hard time. To the public, firefighters were heros while the police had to live with a negative image dispersed by the media.

Ten minutes passed as Detective James sped along Avenue road. His Camaro fishtailed as he made the turn and drove the vehicle into the underground lot. He quickly parked his car and leapt from his seat. Locking the vehicle, he glanced at the foreign imported cars as he made his way to the door of the gym. There were fewer American cars these days, and his seemed to be the last of the vintage models. He wondered when the Canadian government would pull the plug on the American gas guzzlers? There was much concern expressed in the daily newspapers about gas consumption and environmental pollution.

Detective James pushed through the large glass doors as he made his way into the Bloor Athletic complex. Smiling at the attendant, he flashed his membership card then walked into the change room. He deposited his bag in a locker and walked into the gym. Detective James could see his friend weaving back and forth near the canvas bag. With each jab, the bag moved backward. Tod continued to punch at the heavy canvas surface working his fist into the body of his imagined opponent.

"Tod are you ready for that run?" he asked. The auburn haired man turned and starred at the cop as he removed his leather gloves. Detective James expected a tirade of abuse.

"I was wondering when you would get here?" he said.

Detective James smiled as he shrugged his shoulders. His embarrassment was short-lived. Tod Miller led the way though the gym and up the staircase into the warm moist air of the summer morning. Reflexively, both joggers glanced upward at the sky. It was going to be a hot one. The weatherman had predicted another muggy day in Toronto. They usually were right, but Detective James thought they were nothing more than parrots without honest skills.

"Sorry I was late this morning. You probably heard the news about the guy I killed last night. I had to go down to the station and file a report and didn't get out of the place until 2:00 a.m. The press are going to have a good time with this one. When I got home last night, I downed a couple of shots of brandy. I guess I must have overdone it because I sure feel groggy today. The Special Investigation Unit is going to be all over me in about two hours time. Don't believe what you hear in the news, the rapist had it coming. He had a gun pointed at one of the constables when I fired. He wouldn't drop his gun so I put one last round into his head. He shouldn't have raped the girl in the first place. Anyway, the press are going to make it look like I gunned him down. They will probably bring up all my past cases. Its not my fault the criminals are going down. Its my job and the public are demanding protection. I checked his record on CPIC. He had a string of convictions for sexual assault, armed robbery and drug offenses. The way I look at it, I did the criminal justice system a favour," he said as he smiled.

Silence fell over the two joggers as they made their way up Bloor Street toward the park. The resonating sound of their shoes slapping against the pavement broke the silence. Detective James could hear the deep breathing of his friend. He could sense his pulse surging as the tempo of the run increased. Tod was setting a quicker pace than usual, he blurted out some quick statements between gulps of air.

"I can't take the shift work anymore Frank! I've been putting up with all kinds of crappy hours and they still won't put me on steady days. I've got to get out soon. The job is starting to drive me crazy," blurted Tod. The two friends had known one another since Maplewood High. This was the first time he had heard Tod's emotions surface. The pace once again regained its tempo. Detective James listened carefully to the words of his friend. He knew the pressure of being a cop was also getting to him. The chief expected every crime to be solved quickly and the press harassed police officers when something went wrong. Detective James had been hired by the Metro force right after completing his training at the Academy. He had been a police officer for 20 years. He had advanced quickly to his present position but had remained at the rank of Sergeant because none of the higher ranked officers had retired.

The tempo continued once more and only the echo of shoes slapping the concrete was audible. Detective James wondered whether he could hold the pace. He could feel the aching in his oblique muscles as he fought to maintain the stride. Concentrating on his inner thoughts, he was able to block the excruciating pain in his lower abdomen. Through his blurred vision, he could see the building in the distance. Tod quickly bolted ahead with only a hundred yards remaining. Detective James could only watch as the distance between them increased. The officer thought back to his school days at Maplewood High. No one had ever beaten Tod on the track. His friend had won the All Ontario track meet and was destined to be one of Canada's finest runners since Harry Jerome. He often wondered why Tod had refused the scholarship to the University of Toronto. From what he had pieced together, it seemed that his friend didn't have the competitive academic drive. As Detective James reached his destination, he could see Tod leaning against the building stretching his hamstring muscles. Sweat glistened on his friend's brow. Detective James was still gasping loudly.

"Thanks for the run Frank. I needed some competition," said Tod.

"Who are you kidding? I will never give you competition. I could barely complete the jog at the pace you were running," said the cop.

"Let's just say I'm a demanding trainer," replied Tod. The two runners walked into the athletic complex and headed in the direction of the change room. They quickly removed their damp clothing and sauntered into the washroom. After a quick shower, they entered the sauna and positioned themselves on the upper seat. The smell of warm Cedar wood permeated their nostrils. Once more they would enjoy the comfort of the moist heat.

Frank James had been raised on the Onaping River First Nation Reserve. During his childhood, he had gotten use to the ceremonies. His favourite ritual was the sweat lodge. He had learned to savour the warmth and cleansing of the hot humid cedar. On his solo canoe trips, he often built his own small sweat lodge and carried heated stones from the fire pit into the enclosure. From a small pail, he poured the river water on the rocks as he meditated and reflected on his life. Detective James had learned to appreciate his culture and often returned to his small cabin on Lake Onaping. When he wasn't fishing or canoeing, he would spend his time visiting his elderly adoptive parents.

"Looks like we beat the crowd. I feel a little light headed but soon the endorphins should kick in, then I'll feel like a million bucks. At least, I'll be ready for the crap that's going to fly at the precinct this morning. Can you believe the comments on the morning news? They made it sound like I had murdered a defenceless civilian. I've got a feeling the chief is going to come down heavy on me this morning. So what if I've got a track record for kills. All the ones I killed over the years had it coming. No one asked them to come to Toronto and create problems. I was hired as a cop to do a job and that is exactly what I have done. I'm really looking forward to my upcoming vacation. I promised my parents I would take them up the Onaping for some pickerel fishing. I'll take them to the special place I told you about and build a sweat lodge with them. We need to reflect on my sister's death. Ever since her death, they have been having a tough time. We still can't figure it out. She was as healthy as a young deer and out of nowhere she gets breast cancer. After the diagnosis, she only lasted 10 months", he stated calmly. The two joggers had been in the sauna for ten minutes. The heat was becoming unbearable, Detective James grabbed his towel and lunged for the door.

"See you tomorrow morning, I'll try to be here on time," he stated. Frank James cooled his body under the shower and quickly returned to the change room. The sauna had released his inner spirit. His endorphins had been activated by the run, and his mood was elevated. He felt good about himself as he put on his suit. His wet jogging clothes were tossed into his duffle bag. He nodded at the desk attendant as he passed her on the way out of the building. Detective James always felt good after a workout. Without his daily exercise, he knew his job would be a lot tougher. Most of the older cops in his unit were overweight and didn't seem to take any pride in their physical condition. He knew some of his fellow officers were heading for a coronary unless they corrected their poor eating habits. Detective James was not going to leave his job in a coffin. He had plans to retire and return to Northern Ontario. He would only venture south to spend his winters in the Bahamas. He could pursue his favourite hobby in the warmth of the southern coastal waters. Then in the spring, he would return to the boreal forests and stay until he completed the annual moose hunt. He would not let his job as a Metro cop destroy his retirement plans.

Detective James left the gym. He walked briskly toward his car and got in. Deep in thought, he made the trip to the precinct with no recognition of his surroundings. He walked from the parking lot and cautiously picked his way up the stairs. As he edged through the opened doors, he could feel eyes riveted on him. No one said anything, but he knew what they were thinking. The young smiling secretary greeted him with an all too familiar sneer. He knew from her patronizing mannerisms trouble was about to fly in his chief's office.

"Where's the chief?" he asked politely.

"Go right in Sergeant James. They're waiting for you," she said snidely. They? It sounded like this was execution day. Sergeant James mulled over the facts in his mind. He would tell them everything. He would lay the facts on the table without any suppositions. He opened the door and walked toward his commander's desk. Sergeant James thought he recognized the man sitting next to the Police Chief, but was uncertain of the other man on the left.

"I've just read your report and the one filed by Constable Blackburn. I'd like to give you a royal chewing out but his report supports your actions. According to Blackburn, you saved the lives of four people last night. I thought we'd get bad media coverage on this one but it looks like public sympathy is starting to favour us. I got a call from the Toronto Woman's Alliance this morning, you know the group I'm talking about. They write editorials in the newspaper about the lack of support for women in this community. They want to give you a plaque for your bravery last night. They are calling you a hero, and a champion of woman's rights. Their president wants you to give a talk at their upcoming convention. I'm not big on the feminist faction but this one might be good for the department. I'm giving you the time off to attend, but I want a copy of your speech before you give it. I know you can be a little brash, I don't want you offending anyone. Also, you will be getting a commendation for bravery from this department," stated the police chief.

"You probably know Superintendent Elliot of Special Investigations RCMP," he said. Sergeant James stepped forward and firmly shook hands with the respected official.

"Sergeant James, I understand you were on the scene yesterday at the Jobin homicide and are in charge of the investigation. Two terrorists were killed early this morning in their attempt to harm Jonathan Richardson, president of the Panax Corporation. His personal bodyguard provided me with the details. Richardson's brother-in-law, Dr. Milano with the New York branch of Panax was assassinated yesterday. We have some leads on the operative, but are unsure why the terrorists wanted Richardson, Jobin and Milano out of the way. We're not sure what they are after? We have been in contact with the New York Police Department and the FBI. They have a man in custody. He is alleged to have targeted Dr. Milano. The ballistics indicate the bullets killing Jobin and Milano, came from the same gun.

The assassin is apparently linked to the European Liberation Order. They are a mercenary group, who hire out their services. The

FBI had been following a man linked to the European Liberation Order. He was in contact with a radical group known as the American Liberation Order, but vanished shortly after landing in New York. The two terrorists killed at the Panax Corporation were members of the American Liberation Order. The guy in custody in New York, has been linked to the Jobin and Milano homicides. He was shot after he made the hit on Dr. Milano. They are going to interrogate him in a couple of days and provide us with some data. I'd like you to work with Sergeant Cormick," said the RCMP superintendent. Sergeant James stepped forward and shook hands with the RCMP officer.

"Sergeant James! We want you on this case because of your ability to solve crimes. The criminals we're after, use extremes in their operative. We want them in custody or taken out of action. I have reviewed your file with your chief and understand you have killed 30 criminals in the line of duty during your 20 years with the Metro police. You are to act with extreme prejudice. Do you understand what I am saying?" asked the RCMP superintendent.

"Count me in!" responded Sergeant James.

"I understand you have contacts in this city? Maybe your associates can assist us with this matter? Our unit is assigned to International matters. Recently, we received a tip from one of our undercover agents. He filled us in on the American Liberation Order. They're involved in terrorist and subversive acts. It took our agent about two years to infiltrate the American Liberation Order. About a week ago he vanished. I'd like to think he is involved in some covert operation and is out of the country. My gut feeling leads me to believe they discovered his identity. The last we heard from him, was his report informing us the assassins were coming to Toronto to make a hit. The mercenaries entered Canada about the same time Dr. Jobin was murdered. Dr. Milano was killed a day later and you already know about the attempt on Jonathan Richardson. There has to be a connection. I have a feeling something big is in the works. The Panax Corporation operates on a 10 million dollar yearly budget. They receive their funding from environmentalists. Essentially, the Panax organization is a thorn in the ass of any large corporation involved in environmental hazards. They launch civil litigations against industries responsible for releasing toxic wastes into the environment. They get injunctions on industrial corporations and use legal action to shut them down. Two of the administrative officers at Panax have been murdered? We would like to know the motives for the contract killings? We hope to obtain some information when the New York assassin recovers from his wounds. Richardson mentioned he would provide us with data from the Panax files. We hope to find something buried in the paperwork. Maybe it will shed some light on this case. That's all we have to go on at this time," said Superintendent Elliot.

"When do we start?" inquired Sergeant James.

"I like your enthusiasm." The balding heavy-set man retrieved a brown file folder. He released the elastic band and removed documents, a computer disc and a video tape. He returned the plastic band to its position and quickly collapsed the brown folder. He handed the file to Sergeant Cormick.

"Are you ready to start this investigation?" asked Sergeant Cormick.

"Let's get out of here and get this case solved," responded Sergeant James. The door shut loudly behind as they exited from the police chief's office. Frank James looked over at the sneering secretary as he left the office.

"You should have told me I was getting a commendation Mary! I would have dressed for the occasion," he said flatly. The secretary stared at Sergeant James with a bewildered cow-eyed expression. She wondered why he was smiling? Hadn't the police chief given him disciplinary measures for his offensive tactics. Hadn't Sergeant James killed a man?

The two detectives entered Sergeant James office and closed the door. The documents were spread out on his desk. Sergeant James took the CD and inserted it into the computer. He activated his Delwo 5000 and used his mouse to open the program. He positioned the computer so Sergeant Cormick could see the screen. Pictures of the terrorists, affiliated with the American Liberation Order lit up the screen. The names of the men were quickly printed beside the photographs.

"How long has Emerald Lee been involved with the European Liberation Order?" asked Sergeant James.

"We know for sure he's been in three countries when political figures were assassinated. This guy is good at his trade. He slips in undetected, does his job and disappears without a trace," said Sergeant Cormick.

"He must leave some evidence behind," queried Sergeant James. The police detective paused for a moment as he closely inspected the photographs. He wondered what attracted people to the killing profession? He questioned whether it was the money or the homicidal impulse that drove them. The lanky FBI officer studied the photographs. Staring at the pictures he was unaware of his right hand unconsciously caressing the glock automatic in his holster. He thought back over the facts. His friend had been assigned to the case. The last they heard from him was the call made from Montreal one week prior. With each passing day, the RCMP officer knew it was just a matter of time before they uncovered the body. Sergeant Cormick sipped the pungent black liquid in his cup, then looked up at the metro cop.

"This case has taken on some personal meaning for me. My partner was closing in on the mercenaries. They likely discovered his identity and silenced him. We haven't heard from him in over a week," he said.

"Emerald Lee is a master of identities. From the pictures here, you'd think he was five different people.

I'll be interested in the interrogation. They should be able to get some answers out of him as long as they don't mess it up," said Sergeant James.

CHAPTER 7

A week had passed since the sniper's attack on 34th Street. Detective Brown had been impatient to start the interrogation of his prisoner, but even murderers had rights. He had to wait for the physician's approval. A report had been filed but the information still had not been received. Impatient, Detective Brown marched into the office of Forensic Investigation Unit demanding an update on the latest information regarding the assailant. As he waited in the doorway, he glanced into the hallway. He eyed two uniformed cops as they dragged in a well dressed suspect. "A pimp," Brown muttered. He would have enjoyed interrogating this guy. Detective Brown didn't like men who sold women on street corners. It had been seven years since his promotion from the beat. As he looked at the policemen struggling with their quarry, he felt relieved to be in homicide. A uniformed cop just wasn't safe anymore. Maniacs were always looking for easy hits. If everything worked out as planned, he'd be moving to the next level of the organization. The captain was retiring and Detective Brown had solved more cases than anyone else on the force. He would be in line for a promotion.

Detective Brown waited patiently and was finally handed the report on Emerald Lee. He inspected the file. Emerald Lee had graduated with a diploma from a Technology program at the Upper State College. From what Brown read in the file, there were no living relatives. The suspect had been charged for some minor infractions including traffic violations and unpaid parking tickets but other than these misdemeanours, he had no felony convictions. Detective Brown thought it odd the sniper had never served time in a federal penitentiary. He was still awaiting the Interpol report. There was a notation in the file indicating Emerald Lee was suspected of having fought as a mercenary soldier in a country hostile to the United States of America. Detective Brown realized he was not up against a psychotic maniac but a professional killer. The idea made him feel uneasy. He wondered why the sniper had fired on the businessman? He would do more checking, there had to be a connection? If Emerald was a professional killer, Detective Brown wondered why he hadn't left quickly after the hit? A number of questions remained unanswered. He had read the report filed by the FBI agent who was at the scene of the crime. It still wasn't clear why the agent had been there? Detective Brown would speak with Captain Smith and attempt to get more answers. Someone was screening the information. Detective Brown knew he wasn't getting the complete story, there had to be more data on the killer.

The sniper was in maximum security at the Clinton Correctional Facility. Anonymous threats had already been made on the killer's life. Citizens of New York city were beginning to rise up against crime in the city. When police officers were caught in the crossfire, retaliatory remarks were often expressed by the city's fringe members. Detective Brown knew it hadn't always been this way. Bystander apathy had prevailed for many years. It was after the study by the famous social psychologists Latane and Darley and the published report in the New York Times, the city had undergone a metamorphosis. New York had come of age, and those in control of the anti-crime organizations were influencing the masses to rise up against crime. The Continental Rifle Association had come into its own element and many of its influential members had convinced the civilians of the country to take up arms against the criminals. Constitutional claims and the right to bear arms was parroted in their speeches. It was shortly after the terrorist attack on the Twin towers, the mood of the country had changed. When an officer died in the line of duty, citizens rallied and responded with demands for violence against the perpetrator. September 11 had changed it all. The police departments weren't condoning the actions of its citizens, but weren't opposing the notion either.

Some of New York's finest citizens had sworn revenge on the recuperating assailant. Twelve armed guards all members of the tactical unit had been assigned to protect Emerald Lee according to the New York Times. Detective Brown snorted at the newspapers' exaggeration. He knew there had to be a motive for the occurrence on 34th Street. He hoped to unravel the case and obtain some answers. It would give him the leverage he needed for a promotion. The newspaper article suggested Emerald Lee was a professional hit man. From what Detective Brown had uncovered, Dr. Milano didn't appear to have any connection to organized crime. The sniper seemed to have acted like a killer flipped out on drugs, when they moved in on him after the assassination. In Detective Brown's mind something just didn't wash.

Leaving Precinct 14, Detective Brown made his way through the crowded streets. As he descended the stairs to the subway, he read the graffiti miring the concrete walls. He threw his coin into the receptacle and entered the subway transit. People stared blankly ahead, their eyes did not connect with his. Zombie like, they were transfixed in their own consciousness. He had read the articles by Lorenz and Eibl-Eibesfeldt. According to the theorists, the message was in the non-verbal cues. It was clear to Detective Brown, citizens fared best when they displayed the proper body language. The media was getting the message across. To prevent acts of aggression, civilians were told to avert their gaze from the eyes of onlookers. A civilian should avoid eye contact at all costs. Animal researchers had agreed the underlying factor to all acts of aggression was eye contact. This caused perpetrators to release an instinctive aggressive response. Detective Brown had learned the theories in his criminology classes. He knew most citizens who lived in New York didn't have much education beyond their senior matriculation diplomas. They had likely read the articles in the New York Times or seen the reports on television. They had learned the best way to avoid aggressive confrontation was by minimizing eye contact with strangers. Deep in thought, as he reflected on the vagaries of the research on aggression, Detective Brown was not aware of his surroundings and only glanced upward as the subway train came to a stop. He spontaneously rushed through the doors, before they closed on him.

Ascending the stairs of the subway corridor, Detective Brown glanced across the street at the super jail. It had been built in the outer area of the city. The Clinton Correctional Facility was a misnomer. It was not a facility but the best fabricated super jail in New York. It was constructed to house the most undesirable criminals in the city. At the core of the jail was the maximum security division. Special segregation units were developed within the bowels of the jail to warehouse, evaluate and classify the offender populations who walked through the doors of incarceration. Within these inner walls, the criminally deranged were held. Treatment units were created to deal with the criminally insane, sex and assaultive offenders. Psychiatric criminals were not mixed with the others. Some units were created to jail the populations who were beyond the realm of treatment. From the reports he had read, Detective Brown knew the correctional officials were finally beginning to see the light. They had envisioned an incarceration policy which aimed at countering crime. Many of the inmates at Clinton Correctional were assigned life sentences with no chance of parole. They would never leave the facility alive. The death penalty had been revoked in the state of New York and this was the only way of ensuring the most dangerous of the offenders would never harm another member of society. Aggressive homicidal psychopaths would never see daylight again. They would meet their demise in segregated isolation. Detective Brown was satisfied with the new correctional facility developed by the politicians. The crime control policies made his job a little easier knowing aggressive felons would never be released onto the streets of New York.

A burly police officer glanced upward at Detective Brown as he made his way through the heavily plated entrance door of the Clinton Correctional Facility. He asked Detective Brown for identification before he would allow him through the next set of doors. Detective Brown stepped forward to have his Iris scanned and biometric thumb print read. He waited patiently until the data was entered into the computer and a copy of the information spit out by the laser printer. The hard copy was placed in a separate file and classified as Incoming Professional Visitor. Detective Brown felt relieved by the competence of the staff at the Clinton Correctional. They were a sharp contrast to the incompetent officers who still worked at Precinct 14.

Detective Brown slowly made his way through the corridors of the facility and entered the cell block which housed Emerald Lee. The assailant was eating soup when he arrived. Detective Brown entered the room and sat across the table, bullet proof glass separating him from the assailant.

"My name is Detective Brown, I have a few questions to ask you," he calmly stated as he looked through the plate glass window at the assailant. Emerald Lee looked over at the cop and continued slurping the thick green liquid in his bowl.

"We know you are responsible for the shooting of two police officers and ballistics match up with the bullets extracted from the two dead businessmen. I know you're not psychotic. I have data to show you are linked to a mercenary group hostile to the policies of the United States," he stated. Detective Brown was surprised at his own aggression as he barked out the information. He knew Emerald Lee just wasn't worth the time he had to spend on this case. He would have preferred to use his own justice system.

"I don't have to talk to you or anyone else. My defense counsel was here today. He said I didn't have to answer any questions which could incriminate me. You know, I'm the kind of guy who would love to answer your questions, but I'm not talking, unless my lawyer is here," Emerald Lee grinned.

Detective Brown hated the legal system. It was always putting snags into his work. The lawyers were using legal jargon and technicalities to uphold the law, even when they knew their client was guilty? It was one big game, a bad play with poor actors, thought Brown. He could feel his blood pressure rising. He wanted to drop Emerald where he sat but they had already confiscated his weapon at the front door.

"Maybe you don't realize what you did last week. You gunned down two cops, and a businessman. Don't you realize what that means?" asked Brown.

"Yea, I do. That means I'm losing my accuracy with a rifle," replied Emerald. Detective Brown was not shocked by the impulsiveness of the assailant's response. He scanned the room for video monitors and looked over at the doorway to make sure no one was listening.

"If I had my way, I'd give you some justice right here, right now. What gives you the right to shoot down people in cold blood?" he asked.

"I'm not any different than a soldier. Don't snipers shoot defenceless people in war? What about Vietnam, the Gulf War and Iraq? Haven't soldiers wiped out civilians?" Emerald paused, watching Brown carefully.

"That's all I need, philosophical horseshit from a madman," he muttered. He was wasting his time. Detective Brown knew Emerald Lee would not be giving up any information. He gave the incarcerated assailant a cold stare and walked from the room.

"You've got a clever one in there. Watch him carefully," he said to the guard. The correctional officer nodded. He knew the prisoner was capable of anything. He had guarded many in his time, but this one was different.

Detective Brown left the jail and made his way back to the precinct. Entering the building, he ignored Martinelli as he passed him on the staircase. He knocked at Captain Smith's door and walked in.

"Captain Smith, I don't want you to get the wrong impression, but that maniac we have in Clinton Correctional Facility won't cooperate. It's impossible to get anything out of him," he said irately. Captain Smith glanced up through semi-bifocals and for a brief moment looked mildly annoyed at Brown's impertinence.

"I understand detective. We know this is going to be a tough one. I was talking with his lawyer today. Judge Heron has ordered a psychiatric assessment. The doctors at the facility assure us a psychological examination would allow us to know whether he is insane. From the way he acted, they feel he may be psychotic," said the captain.

"I agree he appears to be psychotic. But I just talked to Emerald Lee about thirty minutes ago, he's just as rational as you or I. He shows no more remorse for his crime than a kid does for taking cookies. This guy is not like the other weirdos at Bellevue," responded Brown.

"The court feels a thirty-day judicial order will be sufficient to psychologically assess him. I have faith in the new techniques being developed to evaluate these criminals. It's too bad we didn't have the skill a few years ago. It probably would have made my job a little easier. At one time, it was us against the lawyers. We'd try to bring these maniacs to trial, but with a bright lawyer, the offender just walked. These new Forensic people have helped us out more than once. I can recall a case in Chicago last year where a guy acted as a contract killer for the syndicate. As a result of psychological evidence provided by a forensic psychiatric team, the judge sentenced the offender to a mental institution for life. He's still there and will probably never get out," said the captain.

Detective Brown had his own opinion on justice. There was no sense appearing prejudiced, it might impede his promotion. He left the office and returned to his desk. He would have to dig up more evidence. The psychiatrists would probably do an assessment on Emerald Lee and use some psychological jargon to evaluate his condition. Then, he'd get better and would be released on a not guilty by reason of insanity plea. Detective Brown wanted more justice than the half-assed ivory tower bookworms could provide. Lee deserved the electric chair. Much to Brown's dismay, capital punishment had been eliminated in the state of New York. Detective Brown was determined to bring the assailant to justice.

CHAPTER 8

He didn't like it. Why were they moving him? Emerald Lee had been thinking about an escape. The attendants strapped him into a wheelchair. Two burly cops with bad breath, watched his every move as the electronic doors were activated and the wheelchair moved forward. If he moved, they'd be on him. It would be better to play along for now. He couldn't move if he had wanted, his stomach still ached from the wound. A second bullet had just missed his larynx. It was lucky for him, because without the use of this persuasive organ, he'd be finished. Some guards sneered at him as they passed him in the hallway. Emerald Lee wasn't sure why people were always talking about him, but he had become accustomed to it over the years.

He didn't see any signs on the walls as they wheeled him into the hallway. Only the sombre stares of correctional officers looked in his direction. After what seemed like ten minutes, his wheelchair was pushed into the medical office and positioned across from the attending physician. Emerald Lee waited patiently as the doctor sifted through the medical charts. After making some notes, the grey haired man stoically looked up. His mouth opened and the words were clearly articulated.

"You have a cerebral haematoma, a blood clot in your brain. When you were shot in the neck, a blood vessel ruptured and the clot travelled to one of the major blood vessels in your brain. I'm surprised you haven't shown any ill effects yet? We have scheduled you for surgery at the Bingham Neurosurgical Centre. They have a neurosurgeon who is specialized in the removal of blood clots. I consulted with him just before you arrived in my office. He has scheduled you for surgery this week. We are moving you out of this facility immediately. You will be at Bingham for at least two weeks. The medical team will ensure you are out of harms way before you are returned here. Do you have any questions?" asked the doctor.

Emerald Lee stared blankly at the doctor but did not show any change in composure. In the depth of his mind, the plan was already hatched. A chance for escape had presented itself and the hospital was his way out of this nightmare. He would plan his escape route as they transferred him to the facility. If his scheme worked, he would be out of custody in a week. Emerald Lee smiled at the doctor and thanked him for the diagnosis. The guards quickly wheeled him out of the Infirmary. As the last metal door closed behind him, his escape plan was reaching fruition.

Two police officers and three guards escorted him to the awaiting ambulance. They lifted him inside and strapped him to the stationary stretcher. Emerald Lee stared at the seams running along the upper surface of the cab of the ambulance. The officers sat beside him as the vehicle sped along First Avenue. The vehicle turned into a driveway at Bingham Neurosurgical Centre. As they removed him from the ambulance, his leg made contact with the metal door. A pain jolted up his side, Emerald cursed the guard. The police officers told him to shut his mouth or else they would shove their night sticks down his throat.

The prisoner was moved onto a ramp at the rear entrance to the medical centre and brought in through the back door. Attendants stared at him and looked down at the familiar orange jump suit. Emerald Lee looked up at a young nurse and gave her a wink. She seemed embarrassed and quickly averted her gaze, looking into the opposite direction. The neurosurgery unit was on the third floor. The elevator quickly ascended to the upper level. In his mind, Emerald knew it would be easy escaping from the hospital. He would wait for the right moment, then make his move. As they pushed his chair into the surgical wing of the hospital, his gaze fixed upon the zombie-like figures with bandaged heads marching past him. The patients stared blankly into space as they followed the orderly. Emerald had seen some television shows about head trauma. He remembered the documentary on lobotomies. A chill ran down his spine. A paranoia overtook him as he thought about the experiments they had performed on patients in mental health facilities. Emerald Lee wondered if they were going to attempt their experiments on his brain? He had heard the horror stories. Medical facilities often recruited prisoners in their attempt to perfect procedures. Emerald Lee wondered if he would be subjected to one of these experiments? He would question the doctor? If he did not get the right answers, he would refuse the surgery.

His eyes fixed on the patients as they continued to shuffle past him. Emerald Lee wondered whether their odd behaviour was a residual effect of the surgery or merely a by-product of the drugs? Either way, he knew their brains were not responding well and they seemed to be in the land of oblivion. Recently, he had seen a movie in a bar on 35th Street, the hero had received a frontal lobotomy for acting out on the ward. He never made it out of the hospital after the operation.

Looking into the hallway, Emerald could see the patients following every command of their leader. They showed little capacity for thinking on their own. A sudden fear overwhelmed him. Would he end up like these mindless morons? Patients continued their shuffling past him as the guards stood close by. An orderly talked to one of the guards quietly so he could not he overheard. It had to be drugs, thought Emerald. He would refuse any drug they tried to give him. Hadn't frontal lobotomies been outlawed? Emerald wondered about the reason for his referral to Bingham? He hadn't been experiencing any headaches. Why was he here? Prison had seemed more appropriate. He hadn't been talking to visions in burning bushes or hearing his name called by imaginary strangers. He had just shot some people. Shouldn't he be at the Clinton Correctional Facility?

A sign on the wall near the nurses' station caught his attention. He glanced upward at the bold black letters indicating the room off to the left was the neurosurgical operating room. Everything was moving too fast, he needed more time to plan his escape before they put him under and performed the operation. If something went wrong during the surgery, he might not have the thinking ability needed to plan his escape. Maybe this was only a nightmare and he hadn't awakened from his sleep? He pinched his arm and realized this was not a dream, but a part of his reality.

A nurse approached as he was moved into a private room. An orderly locked the door. Emerald Lee studied the heavy metal door with the double set of locks. It would be difficult escaping from this place. The officer handed the nurse a file. After taking some notes, she thanked him and signalled the orderly to move Emerald Lee onto the bed.

"My name is Mrs. Edmons. I'm in charge of this unit. While you are with us, there are certain rules you must follow," said the plump aging lady. She briefly outlined the situation to him, then mentioned he would have to wear a blue jogging outfit. Emerald made a comment about being unable to jog in his present condition. She showed no facial reaction. He decided to listen, knowing it would be advantageous to cooperate. He would be moved to the Forensic Unit. She informed him he would be evaluated prior to and shortly after his recovery from the operation. The nurse briefed him on the court's decision to have him placed on a judicial order for psychiatric evaluation while he was at the medical centre. Everything would be completed prior to his return to the Clinton Correctional Facility.

"Our job is not to judge you for your crime. We will leave that to the courts. What we want to do is assess your present state of mind. Do you have any questions?" she asked.

"Why have they brought me to this unit anyway? Couldn't the surgery be performed elsewhere? Shouldn't I be returned to the correctional facility right after I recover from the operation? I'm a criminal, not some kind of nut!" he responded.

"This is not a psychiatric hospital. People who have committed criminal offenses and need medical attention are brought to this hospital. You have a blood clot which needs to be removed. We have the neurosurgical team who can perform the operation. Afterwards you will be evaluated by our psychiatric team to ensure you are well," she responded.

"What about those zombies I saw marching around in the hallways? Are they here for a short time?" he asked.

"As I mentioned earlier, while you are here, your behaviour will determine what happens to you. Our program is structured to allow more freedom when you comply with the rules. A psychiatric team will be interviewing you in order to get an idea of your present clinical status. It would be wise to cooperate with them since their report will be sent along with ours to the court," she added. Emerald Lee had no further questions. An orderly wheeled him out of the evaluation room and down to a door marked Hygiene Area. A husky attendant opened the door and motioned them to enter.

"Alright Mr. Lee, into the shower!" grunted the burly attendant. He gave Emerald a bottle of creamy lotion and led him toward an empty stall. Emerald stepped in but stiffened as the cold water saturated his spine. He was just about to scream obscenities at the attendant operating the water flow, when the warmth embraced him.

"Lather up in there!" said the guard.

"Probably thinks I have a disease," thought Emerald as he worked up a thick layer of white suds. Five minutes passed, then Emerald climbed out of the shower. Another orderly changed the dressing on his wounds.

"Put this on!" ordered the husky attendant. Emerald stared at the baggy pants and sweat shirt. The same orderly wheeled him back to a lock up cell. A group of patients were playing cards in the locked cell across from him. A nurse approached and introduced herself. She showed him the chart which the head nurse had talked about. From the list of activities she read to him, he knew he'd be under a great deal of pressure to conform to the rules. Emerald didn't like the idea, but decided to cooperate. It would make things easier on him. He was sure there would be times he could beat the system.

Within an hour, three doctors approached and introduced themselves. He couldn't understand why they were so friendly. Perhaps they were better at his game than he was? He had just murdered some people and the staff were treating him like an old friend. It had to be a trick to break down his defenses. He would have to watch them. From his locked range, he could see a kitchen worker pushing a food cart into the dining area. An aroma filled the hallway. A nurse told the patients their meal would be delivered to their cells. A suspicious-looking patient looked out at him from a cell on the opposite side of the corridor.

"I've heard all about you. There was an article in the paper the other day describing you as dangerous. You don't look dangerous to me. Did you notice the guy with the long black hair sitting at the table? He's violent. Did you know he killed ten people because he thought they were aliens from Uranus?"

"What brings you here?" asked Emerald.

"I've been here for six months. Something happened to me in Milburn. I was walking along Grand Street when a voice told me to help myself to anything I wanted. I was taking a television from an apartment when I had an urge for a peanut butter sandwich. The cops must have been hungry too, cause they came in while I was eating. They asked me what I was doing, so I told them the story. I guess they didn't believe me. I never tell a lie, so I killed them," he said nonchalantly.

Emerald reassured the patient he believed him. He would have to escape, the patients on the ward were insane. After supper, some talked to him from their cells. One inmate revealed how he'd conned women into his car, then raped them. Emerald wanted to kick in the guy's teeth, but the stitches still hurt. Sexual perverts had always made him vomit. While he interacted with the patients, a camera focused on him and followed his every move. Emerald didn't like the idea someone was always spying on him.

CHAPTER 9

"We've got to stop those idiots from dishing out that anti-cruise literature. I believe in freedom of speech, but the crap their handing out is upsetting a lot of people," said the officer dressed in military uniform. The Prime Minister walked to the window overlooking the Rideau Canal. He paused for a moment, stroked his chin and stood motionless. People strolled along the banks of the canal near the Civilization of Man on the Gatineau side of the river. Briefly, they paused to take pictures of the Parliament Building then continued on their stroll. After a long period of silence, the Prime Minister turned and walked over to his desk.

"They may have a point! Have you ever thought what would happen if one of those missiles hit this city? We'd be annihilated. One minute we'd be standing here, the next minute ashes and rubble. Do you call life worthless? I don't think they're crazy. We're the ones who are mad. We continue to let these things happen. Not a word is said when these issues are raised in Parliament. If politicians only had the common sense to realize the impact of warfare, then maybe we'd get somewhere. I agree some demonstrators go too far, but do the housewives and teachers who demonstrate on Parliament exhibit madness? They are probably saner than you or I. What about the politicians and their myopic opinion on these issues? If only there was a more conventional way of getting out of this mess. We're caught in the midst of an important event. If I could personally do something to stop this, I'd be the first to initiate the policy. We ought to go to the next Geneva Summit and give them our opinion. But it just isn't that easy anymore. Besides, they don't have any more control than I do in these affairs. We my friend are merely spokesmen. They look upon us as the leaders of this country, but others call the shots. We're guilty for letting these things happen without saying a damn word. Only three hundred miles from here, we condone the fabrication of the missile guidance equipment used in missile warfare. You probably read about the fanatics who tried to blow up the plant. We should be thankful the employees were out of the building at that time. They blame me for the cruise missile tests! People are constantly on my back. I get hundreds of emails every day expressing concern about nuclear war. People pleading for their children's lives. Articles on the aftermath of nuclear warfare. Do you think I like reading those damn letters? Threats and harassing telephone calls because they think I am at fault. It's difficult having to face this every day. Little do they realize, I am only their spokesman, the country's representative. If I knew of a better candidate to replace me, I'd gladly step down. But I don't know of one in my party who would be capable of doing the job," said the prime minister.

John Wilkinson looked up from his padded leather chair. He knew the Prime Minister had made a good point. "Will I be going to the Geneva Summit with you next month?" he asked.

"There are few aides who possess the ability to process information at the same level you do. I'd like to know the Americans' strategy! If only we hadn't agreed on the cruise missile test. We should have thought this one through. I realize we need good relations with the States, but this time we may have gone too far. If the arsenal is perfected, it'll be a matter of time before other countries get it. Then every radical group in the world would have access. If it weren't for the RCMP, we'd be in a hell of a mess. It didn't take them long to discover terrorists were involved in the Liddon plant explosion. What next? One has to be paranoid in order to survive. I've recently been informed the RCMP are working with the FBI on a highly classified case. It appears a terrorist group known as the European Liberation Order are planning something subversive in Canada," said the prime minister.

"Do the RCMP know what it involves?" queried the military aide.

"They're not sure. At first they thought it was the sale of arms. But from the information they've recently uncovered, it appears much larger than that. They've been tracking an agent with terrorist connections to the European Liberation group. He recently arrived at the Pearson International Airport. They are attempting to uncover his connections," said the prime minister.

"Why don't they arrest him?" asked the aide.

"It's not that simple my friend. He's not your typical criminal. He merely serves as a liaison between the European Liberation Order and other mercenaries. He was a spokesman for the group, but now has risen to a higher position. It's impossible to arrest a man when he hasn't broken any laws. They would like to bring him in for questioning, but first they want to learn the identities of everyone involved. This terrorist faction deals in classified information, nuclear weapons and strategic air defense. It takes them years to attain their positions of high command. But when the time is right, these moles surface, take the information and leave the country undetected. We don't understand how they get clearance in the first place? Its impossible to catch them in the act. But this time, the FBI and RCMP are on to them," he said.

"Where's the surveillance taking place?" inquired John Wilkinson.

"Sorry John, I can't relay that information to you. It's a classified operation. For all we know, you could be working for the organization," said the prime minister.

"Don't be ridiculous! I've lived in Canada all my life. We grew up together," he said with a hint of annoyance in his voice.

"I know that! But try to convince the people in charge of these operations? Everyone is suspect. Every person has his price. Maybe they just haven't found yours yet?" said the prime minister.

"I know what you're driving at, but I think it's ridiculous," said the aide.

"If you were in my position, I don't think you'd see things the same way. I've read all the facts on this classified case. We're not talking about agents from Russia or any of that nonsense. These are extremists - psychopathic terrorists! Call them anything you want, but they have their price. Someone has found a way to buy them. Money, that's the name of the game. They call themselves mercenaries. I'm talking about bright egocentric men and women who become disillusioned with life and align themselves with these idealists. There are a number of them, just waiting for the chance. Academics, military men, and fanatics waiting for the opportunity to join forces with these professional saboteurs. I can think of ten political time bombs ready to explode if they were in the wrong hands. Everything I've said is classified John. Please keep this information to yourself. I'm sure the RCMP will crack this one any day now. It's just a matter of timing," said the prime minister.

CHAPTER 10

It had been four days since they performed the surgery and he was almost fully recovered. A cold wind howled outside the dormitory window as he looked out from his bed. There were better things to do, than lie around in a hospital bed when he could be planning his escape. It would be overcast for the day. He hoped the psychiatric assessment wouldn't take too much time.

Patients were assembling in their range awaiting breakfast. Emerald watched from his cell. One of the inmates was creating a disturbance again. He wondered when they would move him to seclusion. There were periods in which Tom would slip into a deep depression, at those times he was harmless. The manic periods were beginning again. Emerald considered himself lucky, he did not have a psychiatric disorder.

Everything went according to the rules. If a patient acted out, he was immediately removed and placed into seclusion. No chances were given. He overheard an orderly whisper to a nurse something about "time out for Tom". The staff implemented the program to control the behaviour of the patients. If someone acted out in the dining area, they would miss the meal. The approach seemed to be working by the apparent display of conformity.

Following breakfast, he was taken by wheelchair to a testing room. Emerald Lee was apprised a psychologist would be in shortly. Two muscular orderlies waited with him. Few pictures hung on the drably coloured walls in the office. Finally a door opened and a tall male entered.

"Sorry I'm late," stated the psychologist. The orderlies left the office. Emerald turned and inspected the doctor. Gold rimmed glasses partially hid his face. Brown wavy hair was combed back off his forehead. Emerald wondered what surprise questions would be used in the evaluation. He waited for the attack.

"My name is Dr. Allen. The nurse probably told you I would be giving you some questionnaires to complete. You aren't required to tell me anything about your crime unless you want to. My job is to assess you and provide the court with the information. Are there any questions before we start?" he asked. Emerald didn't answer immediately. He felt uneasy. He had expected a manipulative approach by the cunning psychologist. Would there be trick questions to catch him? He would go along with the testing, but would answer cautiously.

"We will start the session with an I.Q. test," said the psychologist.

"Why do I need to have my I.Q. tested?" asked Emerald Lee. The psychologist replied that it would be used to evaluate his cognitive capacity. Emerald knew there would be loaded questions. Rather than lose privileges, he decided to go along with the evaluation.

"Give me your full name, address, marital status, age and date of birth," began Dr. Allen. Emerald answered promptly. He wanted to get out as fast as he could. Maybe he would still have the chance to watch Double Jeopardy if he hurried. The psychologist asked many questions which had easy answers. Within the hour, the I.Q. test was complete. Emerald asked his score and was told he had done well.

"I'm going to show you some cards. I want you to look carefully at them and give me the first answer which comes to your mind. Let's start with number one. What does this look like?" he asked.

"An angel, I can tell by the wings. It could also be the insides of a woman, at least the shape resembles internal organs", he responded. Other cards were placed on the table in succession. "The second one looks like an explosion of flesh. The head is distorted. Blood is flying in all directions. This card appears to be two dancers celebrating. This one looks like a buzzard. It has a peculiar shape, almost like the bird is tearing at a victim's body. This one looks like an explosion, there is blood and guts flying all over the place. This one appears to be two Indian girls playing, or it could be a pair of dogs ripping at a human carcass. I can see demons in this picture. The next one is a shattered woman, her face has been shot off," said Emerald.

"That's it for the cards, now I want you to complete this questionnaire, unless you're too tired," said Dr. Allen. Emerald asked for coffee.

"How would you like it?" asked the psychologist.

"Black," he muttered. Emerald Lee read the directions. "What if I can't make up my mind?" he asked. The psychologist told him to answer with the first idea which came to mind. Emerald read the questions and checked off the answers.

"Evil spirits possess me at times, what is this supposed to mean?" he mumbled.

"Are you possessed by evil spirits?" responded Dr. Allen.

"What kind of moron do you take me for!" Emerald Lee believed some of the questions had been placed on the test to intentionally mislead him. Dr. Allen sipped his coffee as he watched the patient check off answers. Two hours passed, finally, Emerald put down his pencil.

"Do you have questions about any of the material?" asked the psychologist. Emerald was in deep thought.

"Do I get the results?" he asked. Dr. Allen assured the patient he would provide the results as soon as the tests were scored. Emerald was also informed he would be returning the following day to complete other tests. An orderly entered the room and Emerald Lee was returned to his cell.

Dr. Allen reflected on his interaction with the patient. He had assessed many criminals, but this was his first contact with a contract murderer. Close inspection of the intelligence test showed Emerald Lee had scored in the superior range of intelligence. Very few patients tested on the Forensic unit, had scored in the superior range. The responses to the Rorschach Inkblot were replete with feelings of aggression, impulsiveness and paranoia. Emerald Lee had been obsessed with blood and mutilated corpses. The MMPI would be scored by the computer and the output available later that day. Dr. Allen reflected on the data. Emerald Lee appeared to have characteristics consistent with that of a psychopath. His paranoid tendencies compelled him to be suspicious of others. He probably blamed society for the bad times he had experienced.

The psychologist reflected on the outcome of the surgery. Dr. Moniz had personally informed him there would not he any observable changes in behaviour. The neurosurgery hadn't impaired Emerald Lee's thought processes. The neurosurgeon had implanted the nanochip into Emerald Lee's brainstem just beneath his cerebellum. Dr. Moniz had predicted Lee's behaviour would not be disrupted. When Lee attempted to engage in an aggressive act however, his impulses would be blocked by the program installed on the silicon chip. Lee's aggression would be inhibited. The programmed nanochip would release massive doses of norepinephrine from his locus coeruleus into the basolateral area of Lee's amygdala.

Earlier research by Jose Delgado and Robert Heath had shown electrodes implanted deep into the neural circuitry of the brain could halt aggressive behaviour. The CIA had provided extensive funding to the brain research programs. It was the CIA's intent to use the data to advance military combat. The results of the research were impressive, criminal behaviour could be modified by electrostimulation. Fifty years later, Dr. Moniz had taken the research model to the next level. He had implanted the programmed nanochips deep into the neural circuits of the prisoners' brains. His results had shown aggression could be controlled. Emerald Lee's aggression would be halted in a similar manner, and he no longer would be a threat to society.

CHAPTER 11

"Do we have enough evidence to move in?" asked the thin balding cop.

"No, not yet. You and Sergeant James have done well in your investigation but we still haven't got all the facts. Santi may be wise to the operation. There were five good men following him, but they lost contact in New York. They still don't know how he managed to escape. If we move in now, they may get wise to us and disappear," replied Superintendent Elliot. The captain walked to his filing cabinet, unlocked the drawer and took out a thick file. He thumbed through the material and withdrew an envelope. He returned to the desk and sat in his leather chair.

"Operation Dismantle. Let's see what we've got. Maintain surveillance on the men associated with the European Liberation Order. We have dossiers on their activities in Africa and the mid-East. I'm not sure how they fit in. One is self-employed as a computer analyst. The other is a retired USA Air Force Colonel. We're still not sure about the extent of their operation. Something tells me it's much bigger than Homeland Security has implied. The systems analyst is no ordinary computer programmer. He did his Ph.D. at Berkley and has completed two post doctorates at the best institutes in the States. He has no political affiliations we know of. We've had a man on him for a week. He hasn't made a move since he was contacted by Santi," stated the superintendent.

"What about the Air Force Colonel?" Do you have any information on him?" inquired Sergeant James.

"He's one of the best! Fought in the Gulf War. Had a good hit rate. He received a number of medals for dangerous missions behind enemy lines. He was shot down and spent a few months as a prisoner of war. They returned him to the USA in exchange for military prisoners at Guantanamo Bay. Currently, he works with a shipping firm. We have no information linking him to subversive activity. As far as we know, he has a good standard of living. He doesn't have to rely on outside sources for income. According to the report, he doesn't drink or gamble. I can't understand how he got mixed up in this thing," replied the superintendent.

"What about the period behind enemy lines? Is there a possibility he may have gone over to the other side? When he returned from captivity was there any sign of brainwashing?" asked Sergeant Cormick.

"Good point Ralph! The military psychologist did an assessment on him. According to the report, Colonel Bacstrom was in good mental shape after his return. They ran him through an intensive psychological evaluation, nothing came out of it", said the superintendent.

"I guess we'll just have to wait this one out," added Sergeant Cormick.

"Yes, I'm afraid so. We haven't got much to go on. We're going to have to wait until they make their move," said the superintendent. As he placed the file on his desk, Superintendent Elliot rubbed his brow. He wondered about the subversive activities? A number of questions still lingered in his mind. Were the Americans withholding something? Why had Santi returned to New York immediately after his trip to Toronto? Questions remained unanswered. Now was the time to use the classified number. Superintendent Elliot opened the desk drawer and retrieved the number from a black book. He lifted the telephone from the receiver and dialled the number as he looked at the two men waiting near his desk. The speaker phone was activated so the detectives could hear the conversation.

"This is Superintendent Elliot with the RCMP in Toronto. I'd like to speak to Captain Morand," he stated authoritatively. The superintendent could hear papers being shuffled in the background. Finally, he heard the voice which had become familiar to him over the past month.

"I would like to know what further directives you can provide on Operation Dismantle Captain Morand. We've been watching the suspects but they haven't made a move. What would you like us to do next?" asked the superintendent.

"We're still trying to locate Santi. We know he hasn't left New York. He's expected to make contact with an ELO sympathiser within the next few days. We've got the place staked out. There isn't much you can do at this point. I'd like to meet with you and the men working on this case. Could you come to New York tomorrow? It's important we talk in person," said Captain Morand.

"Yes, that can be arranged. What time?" he asked.

"Ten o'clock Tuesday morning," replied Captain Morand.

"We'll be there," the superintendent responded. He placed the phone on the receiver and returned the small black book to the drawer. The key was inserted and the drawer locked.

"He wants to talk with us. I'll have my secretary book our flights. Do you have any further questions?" asked Superintendent Elliot. The two cops looked at one another and then back at the superintendent. They lifted themselves from the chairs and walked from the room.

CHAPTER 12

Sergeant James looked out from the window of the DC-10. He recognized the familiar landmark beneath them. The peninsula almost appeared like a kidney from their present altitude. The plane would soon be landing. He slowly turned his head toward the men who had become familiar to him over the last two weeks. They'd be meeting with Captain Morand in about an hour to discuss Operation Dismantle. It wasn't often Homeland Security worked in conjunction with the RCMP and CSIS. Little was known of the operation at this point. He wondered whether the captain would provide the information? Once again, Sergeant James glanced at the men, then lightly nudged his partner. Startled from a deep sleep, Sergeant Cormick bolted upright and focused on the person who had disturbed him.

"What is it?" he asked.

"We're almost there, Ralph. You'd better fasten up. Tell Superintendent Elliot to fasten his seatbelt," he said quietly. Just as Sergeant Cormick secured the buckle, the flight attendant's voice broke the stillness of the cabin, alerting the passengers about the landing procedures. Within the hour, they'd be at Captain Morand's office. Sergeant James wondered whether the captain would relay all the details of the case? He wondered why the terrorists were in Canada? It seemed to be an intricate puzzle woven with missing facts.

The DC-10 glided smoothly onto the runway. Tires screeched briefly as the aircraft set down. He could hear the screaming of the brakes, the aircraft quickly decelerated. At the end of the runway, the DC-10 made a left turn and taxied the passengers to the ramp near Terminal One. In a few minutes they'd be on their way to the Homeland Security headquarters. Sergeant James breathed a sigh of relief as he left the aircraft. Being confined in a small space never appealed to him. Sergeant James wasn't claustrophobic, he just didn't like breathing stale air for such a long period.

It was as busy as the secretary said it would be. The hallways seemed endless. Sergeant James and his associates fought their way through the crowded airport corridors and made their way to the luggage area. Almost as quickly as they arrived, the conveyor belt delivered their shoulder bags. Reflexively, they walked toward the customs officer, withdrawing their passports. Two robust men were called over.

"These men would like to talk to you," said the customs officer.

"Who are you?" asked Superintendent Elliot.

"We're working with Captain Morand. I'm Lieutenant Regan and this is Sergeant Strand. We have a car waiting outside. Will you follow us please?" he asked politely. The three men glanced at one another then followed. A large black SUV was parked alongside the curb next to the yellow cabs. Sergeant Strand opened the rear door, and the officers slid onto the plush leather seat. Little was said between them as they drove into the interior of the city.

Sergeant James looked out through the window and found himself mesmerized by the skyscrapers. Although he had seen the Twin Towers on his last visit, he strained hard to visualize the buildings prior to the air attack. The vacant space seemed to reach upward toward the sky. Many had only begun to accept the vacuum of despair as testimony to memories of the fallen victims. Sergeant James watched the driver as he continually checked his rear view mirror. The SUV weaved its way through the heavy downtown traffic. Sergeant James looked out from his window, but did not recognize any of the street names. The vehicle made two sharp left turns then proceeded into an underground parking lot.

"We'll make our way from here," said the driver. No information was exchanged as the two American cops ushered them into up a staircase and toward an elevator. From the corner of his eye, Sergeant Cormick carefully inspected the area. He wasn't sure what to make of the meeting. Why had everything been so secretive? They were dealing with a classified operation, perhaps the operation was a little bigger than the Americans had let on. The elevator door opened and the officers were motioned to follow. Sergeant Strand pressed his thumb against a biometric keypad and the elevator ascended. When they reached the 5th floor, the door opened. In the background they could hear the omnipresent white noise radiating into the hallway. The officers were led through a door and told to wait. A recorded voice asked their identity. A camera fixed itself on the three Canadian cops.

"Please come in," announced a voice. The door slid into a recessed cavity. A secretary smiled at them, as they entered her office.

"Please be seated gentlemen. Captain Morand will be with you shortly," she said. After a minute of silence a door opened to the captain's office.

"I'm Captain Morand. I trust you gentlemen had a pleasant flight. My secretary will be in shortly with some coffee, have a seat." The officers seated themselves to the right of the captain's desk.

"I'll get right to the point. Our agency doesn't typically involve others in its operations. In most assignments we investigate, evaluate and make the arrests. This one however, is a little different. You probably know that Homeland Security was created as a special security unit to investigate terrorism and subversive activity. We received information the European Liberation Order, an organization hostile to the United States of America was planning terrorist activity in New York. The ELO consists of fanatics who render terrorist services, anything from espionage to assassination. They have no particular political ties. Anyone with sufficient money can contract their services. We know of twelve members at the core of their group. They are professional killers. They move in, do the job and vanish from sight. One of these agents is in New York. We don't want to move in on him until we know exactly what he's up to. Your surveillance has proven quite useful to us. At first, we believed they were planning the political overthrow of an African nation. But from the data we've compiled, it's beginning to look more like missile warfare. There are still many questions which remain unanswered. You can be assured, we are digging deep for the facts. We want to know who fronted the operation? I'm convinced as soon as we pick up Santi's trail, we'll be able to get the information. I wanted you here, to impress upon you the importance of this operation," said the captain.

"We have uncovered some interesting facts. The ballistics I received, indicate Emerald Lee was the shooter in the Toronto and New York incidents. He is in custody at the Clinton Correctional Facility. We want to interrogate him but my contact with the Bureau of Corrections and Rehabilitation indicates Lee has just undergone surgery and is still recovering from his wounds. Even criminals have rights these days. Lee is a member of the ELO faction, he is an assassin. We had been tracking him, but he slipped into Toronto and made the hit. When he returned to New York, we had him in our grasp but lost him. Then he made the second confirmed kill. We eventually got him, but some good men died in the process. We're still attempting to unravel the facts. Are there any questions?" he asked. The Canadian officers looked at one another, then returned their stare to the captain.

"Do you have information on the retired Air Force Colonel or the computer expert?" asked Superintendent Elliot.

"The Colonel's record is clean. But he has had contact with a Canadian commander at a military post in Alberta. The RCMP have him under surveillance. The computer analyst has been involved with groups hostile to the American government. We have reports he has had contact with the American Liberation Order. We'll be filling you in on all the details as soon as we receive the facts. Until then, continue your investigation and see what you can uncover. If you have questions at any time, I want you to contact me. You've got the number," said the tall wiry captain.

"Any questions?" asked Superintendent Elliot.

"No, I guess not," replied Sergeant James. Captain Morand stepped forward and shook hands with the three Canadian officers. He pointed to the secretary's office, indicating she would get them a ride back to the airport.

"Why weren't we informed of the RCMP's involvement in Alberta", asked Sergeant Cormick.

"We are doing our part in Ontario, other RCMP detachments are also involved. A thorough investigation is necessary if we are going to root out these saboteurs," was the superintendent's reply. The secretary smiled at the three men as they entered her office. She dialled the number and then hung up the phone. She indicated someone would arrive in ten minutes to drive them to the airport.

CHAPTER 13

Almost two weeks had passed since Emerald's assault on 34th Street. Detective Brown had unravelled little. He was going to the Bingham hospital to evaluate the situation. He wanted some reassurance Emerald Lee was secure until his return to the Clinton Correctional Facility. Lieutenant Brown telephoned Yellow Cab and requested Bert Laberre pick him up. Leaving the headquarters, he gazed up at the overcast sky, then stared at a puddle of water which had collected in a damaged section of the sidewalk. The cab driver pulled up to the curb.

"Bert, drive me to Bingham Neurosurgical Centre," said Lieutenant Brown as he entered the cab.

"Yes sir Lieutenant Brown, you can bet your sweet ass," replied the cabbie. Lieutenant Brown couldn't believe Bert Laberre was succumbing to the lower-class jargon of New York. Detective Brown had been raised in Harlem. It had been painful during that period of his life. Only after his father returned from the Vietnam war, life had gotten better for his family. He preferred not to think of those early days.

"Lieutenant Brown, there is talk on the streets, the sniper is getting off the murder charge because he was nuts at the time," said Bert.

"That's horseshit! Emerald Lee is in custody and has just undergone surgery for the slugs I put into him. I'm on my way to interrogate him right now," he replied. Detective Brown wasn't surprised the press distorted the facts. They always seemed to be looking for sensationalism.

"Sacrament! So you're still working on the case?"

"Yes, I am! Don't believe what you hear unless you check out the source. You'll often find the media tends to distort information. Most of what they tell you is crap," said Brown. Silence prevailed for the next ten minutes as the yellow cab made its way to the hospital. The cab driver asked which entrance he wanted. Lieutenant Brown was unsure, he hadn't been to Bingham before.

"Drive me to the administration building Bert, I'll find my way from there." Detective Brown stepped from the car. Light rain continued to pour from the overcast sky. The hospital appeared desolate and cold. He entered through the foyer and asked the lady at the front desk for directions to the Forensic Unit. She rattled off the information and told him to take the elevator. At the end of the hallway, he could see a guard securing the entrance to the Forensic Unit. He was asked for identification and showed his badge to the guard in the enclosed chamber. Slowly, the door opened to the secure area. Detective Brown passed through two more heavy metal doors. The elevator would take him to the floor housing the patients in Forensics. As he emerged from the elevator, Detective Brown walked toward the door which permitted entry to the Forensic Assessment Unit. A security officer confirmed Detective Brown's identity, then allowed him to pass. As he entered the unit, an orderly was waiting for him.

"I will take you to Dr. Allen's office", he said.

Detective Brown glanced through the small windows on the doors as he walked toward the psychologist's office. The guard stopped abruptly and knocked on the door. They were invited to enter.

"I'm Lieutenant Brown. I have an appointment," he said factually.

"Come in detective! I'm Dr. Allen! I've been expecting you." Detective Brown was surprised by the doctor's appearance. He had expected to see a bearded shrink.

"You look bewildered Lieutenant Brown," stated the psychologist.

"Actually, I thought you would have a beard!" joked Brown.

"Not me Lieutenant Brown, I'm one of the normal guys," replied the doctor. Detective Brown smiled. He appreciated the doctor's sense of humour. Detective Brown glanced through the room. He had expected to see the accepted symbols revealing a man's professional status. But there weren't any diplomas, special awards, ribbons, or pictures of the doctor's family in view. Detective Brown wondered what hidden recesses stored Allen's data?

"Earlier you mentioned wanting to know more about Emerald Lee. Where would you like me to start? I had him sign a consent form, I can disclose the information," he stated.

"What makes him tick?" asked the cop.

"I have just completed a court ordered assessment, the report will be released to the judge. From my assessment, I learned Emerald Lee was an only child, raised solely by his mother. His biological father deserted the family when Emerald was one. His mother later hooked up with a bartender. Apparently the bartender was physically abusive towards Emerald. Mr. Lee experienced numerous problems during his childhood. We obtained his school records. In primary school, there were behavioral reports of Lee being detached and withdrawn. Apparently, he had few friends during his formative years. He did well in high school however, and graduated at the top of his class with an 85% average. After that, he attended college on a scholarship and graduated from a three year program in computer programming and electronics. I should also mention he was a member of the college rifle club," the doctor replied factually.

"You indicated an interest in motive Lieutenant Brown. I've provided you with some detail on his childhood so you could appreciate the type of person we are dealing with. The events which happened during his formative years have moulded him into the type of person he is today. I'm not sure if you have any background in psychology? I administered a battery of psychological tests. His responses showed a host of characteristics including paranoia, impulsivity, antisocial behaviour and schizoid feelings. Clinically speaking, this fellow is a dangerous man. The psychological data indicate Emerald Lee has developed a self-centred approach to life. He has no consideration for others. I have reason to believe his formative experiences have caused Emerald to develop a narcissistic personality style. Lee has been diagnosed as having a psychopathic disorder, he is not treatable", replied the doctor.

"You can't treat him? Does that mean he is insane?" asked Detective Brown.

"Negative! He is not insane and can stand trial for his offenses. From our files, we know this is the first time he's exhibited homicidal behaviour. Past behaviour is a good predictor of future behaviour. Emerald's shooting spree speaks for itself. I have no doubt about his future actions. He will act violently, whether he's provoked or not. I'd like to introduce you to a researcher who's been evaluating Emerald Lee's behaviour on the ward. Let's get her opinion," he stated. Getting onto the ward was like busting into Fort Knox. The door was opened and quickly locked. The Monitor Room was off to the left. Two doors were unlocked and re-locked. The inner room hummed with activity. At the control panel, an attractive middle aged woman activated switches which flashed images onto the video screen. A smile exchanged between Dr. Allen and the woman.

"Lieutenant Brown, this is Dr. Jenny Peterson," said Allen. Dr. Peterson was a tall shapely brunette with dark penetrating eyes partially covered by gold rimmed glasses.

"Jenny, have you noted any interesting behaviour in Emerald Lee?" asked the psychologist.

"He's been exhibiting a peculiar facial tick and some compulsive behaviour. Let me show you the tape," she responded. From the way she fixed her eyes on Dr. Allen, Brown knew Allen was probably intimately involved with her. Fringe benefits thought Brown, some people have all the luck. The camera zoomed in on Emerald, a scar on his forehead seemed quite prominent.

"Our reports indicate Emerald Lee was assaulted by his mother's boyfriend at the age of three. It took thirty stitches to close the wound. The tape rolled forward. They could see Emerald Lee talking with other patients. One of the patients made a remark. Emerald laughed hysterically, but instantly replaced his expression with a sombre look.

"What do you think? Is that typical behaviour?" asked Brown.

"I'm not sure, but from my study of human behaviour, it isn't a good clinical sign. It's almost as though Emerald Lee is in battle. One part of him wants to relax and the other wants control," replied Dr. Peterson. Detective Brown had seen enough, he was convinced Lee wasn't mentally ill. The forensic report would indicate Lee wasn't insane. He would be released from Bingham Neurosurgical Centre and returned to the Clinton Correctional Facility. Lee would be tried and convicted of his offenses. Detective Brown would fulfil his obligation and bring the criminal to justice.

CHAPTER 14

The games-room buzzed with activity. Emerald Lee kept a low profile. Contact existed only when he found it necessary to manipulate others. Having been caught cheating at cards during a tournament, he replied it was only a game. Games were meant to be won or lost. He only played to win, he had told others. Inmates soon learned Emerald Lee was not to be trusted. His twisted logic repelled many of them. Emerald disregarded rules and slyly plotted against those who despised him. He tempered emotions in all, and aligned his enemies and allies the way a child played with toy soldiers. Orderlies and nurses showed caution. Rumour spread of Emerald Lee's contempt. He would soon be leaving the hospital and would be transferred back to the correctional facility. His name surfaced in all crevices of the hospital. Many debated his fate, while others hedged wagers on it. His name grew in potency as they talked of his deeds. It seemed Emerald Lee had masterminded his ill-fated charade.

None of the Forensic staff wanted Emerald Lee on their case load. Finally, they drew lots, the winner would emerge the loser. Alice Holmes forced a toothy grin as she learned of her fate. Alice had been working at Bingham for five years. Some loved her, while others despised her. Those who disliked her did not share her religious beliefs. Alice had been "reborn", she had seen the light. As a follower, she believed it her duty to impart the truth to others. Inmates were easy prey. Distraught and emotionally broken, they sought her help. She fed their needs, nurtured their emotions, then set the trap. Many fell victim and aligned. Others having been cleverly taken in, were too embarrassed to rebuke her.

Alice was convinced she could show Emerald Lee the light and the truth. Given renewed faith, he would charismatically persuade others to the fold. He would be her instrument. Ritualistically, she visited Emerald every day, bringing with her snippets of information about the good book. After reading the testimonies, she believed he would understand. Alice knew from the way he acted towards her, he was changing his ways. Emerald Lee had been under her guidance for almost a week. She was certain he would fall to his knees any day, begging for salvation. Alice would be there to aid him.

A heavy rain poured down into the fenced yard. None of the inmates would be going out for exercise. They would have to remain indoors because of the weather. Tension pervaded throughout the activity room. Emerald needed action, but knew there would be none. As Alice Holmes walked toward him, a scheme had already taken shape in his mind. Emerald approached her and flashed a smile.

"Hello Alice! How are you?" he asked. Alice returned his smile, her retracted lips exposing large protruding nicotine-stained incisors.

"Alice, I was wondering if I could talk to you privately. I've been reading the good book and have been making some serious decisions," he said. She was flabbergasted. A fleeting thought ran through her mind. Was he finally ready? Would he make a commitment?

"Emerald, I'm pleased to hear you are ready. I've always known you would be willing to accept him into your heart some day," she replied. Alice had thought of him as an unfortunate soul who had lost his way. He would soon be leaving Bingham and returning to jail. She would prepare him for the journey. Alice asked the orderly to open the interview room. Emerald's cell was not the place for the initiation. The orderly inquired if she would need assistance to ensure no altercation took place. Alice gracefully declined his offer. She could not believe Emerald Lee would lift his hand against a kitten. He had seen the light. Alice offered him a comfortable chair. Had he not carried a burden most of his life? She would lighten his load.

"I've been thinking Miss Holmes, I would like to change. Until this time, I have never known how to go about it. Having met you, and with your encouragement, I think I can do it," he said. Alice was deeply touched, a moistness came to her eyes. Emerald described his personal experiences, misfortunes and wrong-doings. She was in sympathy.

"I can feel what you're saying. I'm happy it was I who found you. Will you accept him into your heart?" she said.

"Miss Holmes, if you would give me a few seconds to collect my thoughts, I could probably say it. Do you think that you could turn your head for a few minutes? I feel very embarrassed."

"Of course, I realize what you must be going through Emerald." She turned her head and an ominous silence fell over the room.

"Okay Miss Holmes, I think I'm ready." Alice turned and looked at him. He grabbed her, held her romantically, and planted a large kiss on her puffy lips.

"I have seen the light Miss Holmes. Would you like me to show you the way?" he chortled. His boisterous laughter echoed into the hallway. Alice Holmes screamed as she ran from the room. He was in stitches.

Emerald sat in the barren solitary confinement room gazing at the camera which focused on him. His punishment for the act had been detention. They informed him, plans were being made to send him back to jail. The more he thought of his predicament, the more irritated he became. Emerald knew he had to escape. Fifteen days had passed since his arrival and he was heading back to Clinton Correctional Facility. There would be no escape once he returned to jail.

He didn't like people spying on him. Emerald Lee wished whoever worked the camera would stop. It seemed like he had been confined for centuries. Supper was brought to him at the usual hour. The orderly made a few crude remarks but Emerald did not react. Emerald Lee was told he would be returning to the correctional facility as soon as he was finished his supper.

A hundred ideas passed through his mind as he went through his plan. Everything was in order. With one guard at the front and one at the rear, they marched him down the hallway. He was being returned to jail. Emerald ran the plan through his mind. It would work if he could play it right. The echoing footsteps reminded him of marching soldiers. An image of Gestapo police danced through his mind. He would have been of service to them. He cared little for people and considered them nothing but objects to be used and discarded. No one had cared for him during his early years, they had ridiculed and rejected him.

A sense of relief was experienced as he marched through the metal security doors. He greeted the old guard with a friendly smile. As he walked down the hallway, he feigned stomach pains and doubled over. At the same time, he quickly inserted his fingers into his throat. A frothy putrid substance was projected onto the guard in front of him. In disgust, both guards grabbed Lee and led him into a washroom. The room was empty, just as he had expected. He fumbled for some tissue as he huddled over the toilet bowl. Cautiously, he glanced up as he wiped his mouth. The guard turned his head to avoid the revolting sight. Like a cat, Emerald Lee sprung at his victim. The weight of his body riveted the man against the wall. The next blow doubled him. As the head of his rival fell forward, Emerald's knee lifted into his victim's face, sending him into unconscious oblivion. The second guard leaped at him through the door of the stall. Emerald was ready for him and slammed the door against the man's body, sending him to the cement floor. Emerald's shoe made its connection and silence prevailed. As Emerald Lee removed the guard's uniform, he experienced a migraine headache deep in the recess of his brain. A feeling of nausea overcame him and he felt sick to his stomach. As he glanced down at the fallen victims, he vomited. A pain deep inside his brain caused him to shake uncontrollably, making it difficult to dress into the guard's uniform. He tried to regain his composure, but the painful migraine continued to pound in his head. Knowing he had to escape, Emerald Lee fought with the sensations in his head. He opened the bathroom door and cautiously walked out. The guard's security card was used to bypass the electronic codes. By the time the staff realized something had gone wrong, he'd be far from the hospital grounds.

CHAPTER 15

The unconscious bleeding guards were discovered within the hour by one of the orderlies. Detective Brown was notified just as he prepared to leave the station. He quickly put out an APB to all New York precincts. The evening news carried a brief report of the daring escape. Emerald's picture flashed over the television networks. A detailed description was reported in the Times that evening. The escapee's violent nature suggested he not be approached. Police were to be contacted immediately if he was seen.

Lieutenant Brown worked at his desk throughout the night attempting to piece the incident together. The more he contemplated his predicament, the more enraged he grew. He telephoned Dr. Allen and arranged an early morning appointment. The psychologist was waiting when he arrived at the hospital. Dr. Allen appeared perplexed about the situation.

"Emerald should have been watched more closely. I impressed upon the guards the gravity of this situation. I wish those idiots would have taken the necessary precautions," said Dr. Allen. Detective Brown felt the same way. Why had they not personally consulted him prior to the transfer back to Clinton Correctional?

"What do you think he's going to do?" asked Brown.

"As I mentioned on your last visit, Emerald is an impulsive psychopath with violent tendencies. His behaviour speaks for itself. We know he is a killer! I only hope no one gets in his way," responded the psychologist. Dr. Allen had been studying Emerald for the last thirteen days. Lee's only contact with people had been when he manipulated them.

"He's a dangerous psychopath. I have a hunch he will revert to his past behaviour. Emerald's just as impulsive now, as he was when he entered Bingham. If he gets the urge to act out his aggression, he won't be stopped. You had better contact the gun shops in the city. Remember, past behaviour is indicative of future behaviour. If you obtain any information please let me know. I could give you answers more quickly than you could get them from a computer. Besides, your computer is only as good as the programmer who feeds it data. Without the right questions, there's no possible way you can get all the answers," said the psychologist.

Lieutenant Brown hurried from the gloomy building. As he slid into his car, many questions flashed through his mind. Driving from the parking lot, Lieutenant Brown wondered why he hadn't gunned down Emerald Lee when he had the chance.

Dr. Allen walked over to the filing cabinet and inserted the key into the lock. Removing the file, he returned to his desk. He opened the brown manila folder and thumbed through the contents. Inspecting the data, he reflected on the case. The intelligence test indicated Emerald had scored in the superior range, the escaped offender was bright. He would be difficult to locate, unless of course he made a mistake. On the MMPI he was elevated on the psychopathic deviate, paranoia and mania scales. Inspection of the Hare Psychopathy Checklist indicated Emerald Lee was elevated on psychopathy. Dr. Allen thumbed through the data on Lee's tendency for recidivism. The Violence Risk Appraisal Guide showed he had an elevated propensity to act out. Dr. Allen reflected on the information provided by the neurosurgeon. If everything went according to the plan, Emerald Lee would soon show some change in behaviour. The surgical procedure was based on the early experimental work of Jose Delgado and Robert Heath. Dr. Hernandes Moniz had been experimenting with a similar procedure at Bingham Neurosurgical Centre. He had used neurosurgery successfully on many aggressive offenders. Dr. Allen had been asked to join the medical group. He had been allowed access to the clandestine society because of his involvement with the criminal offenders. His psychometric testing had confirmed Emerald Lee's aggressive personality characteristics still existed. The surgical procedure however, would never allow Lee to commit another homicide. The nanochip had been implanted into Emerald Lee's brainstem and wired into his locus coeruleus and amygdala. Whenever the offender's brainstem showed elevated arousal, it would trigger his neural circuitry. A massive release of the neurotransmitter norepinephrine would fire into his basolateral amygdala. Emerald Lee would experience stress and a severe panic attack. This would override his aggressive urges and shut down his tendency for violence. He would never take another human life.

Dr. Moniz had convinced the neurosurgical team of the necessity to go forward with the nanowiring. It would ensure homicidal maniacs would never again be a threat to civilians. Emerald Lee's daring escape was testimony to the success of the surgical implant. He had busted up the guards during his escape, but had not killed them. In time, the nanochip would imprint the information into Emerald Lee's emotional brain and his aggressive behaviour would be controlled. Much like the early experiments on criminal offenders, aggression would cease and the dangerous psychopath which dwelled deep in the brain of Emerald Lee would be silenced.

CHAPTER 16

Forty-eight hours had passed since he'd gone into hiding. Emerald Lee thought about his situation. The vacant building would afford him sanctuary as he worked through the plan. Later, he would attempt to make contact with his associate. His empty stomach growled from lack of food. The dampness of the desolate building penetrated his thin wiry frame. Emerald would have to deal with his misery if he was going to remain free. The damp morning air gripped at him as he crept through the building searching for something he could use as a weapon.

Few inhabitants stirred in this bohemian part of town. The police usually stayed clear of the area. They didn't like being harassed by the derelicts from this section of the bowery. Looking our from his lair, he could see the small neon sign flashing above the restaurant. Emerald crept from the deserted warehouse and crossed to the opposite side of the street. He entered the building. Scanning the empty hallway, he made his way to the washroom. The grimy sink hadn't been washed in months. He rubbed the dispenser soap into his hair and used the greasy substance to comb the stands behind his ears. The dark-rimmed sun glasses he'd removed from the stolen vehicle made him appear older. His new image reminded him of an actor he'd seen in films. He tried to recall the name but could not bring it to his conscious level.

Cautiously, Emerald walked out from the washroom and entered the restaurant. He ordered a coffee from the approaching waitress. The warmth of the smoke filled environment relaxed him, a drowsy feeling gripped his brain. Sipping the beverage slowly, his plan was laid out in his obsessive mind. He would need money and a new identity. Emerald Lee remembered, he barely had enough to cover payment for coffee and toast. When he finished his meal, he left the change on the counter and quietly slipped through the front door. The street was coming to life and derelicts ambled unsteadily along the broken concrete.

The wanted criminal would have to remain in the bowels of the city until he made the necessary contact. He wondered whether the disguise would work. If he could get in touch with Max Winter, the second phase of his plan would be initiated. Emerald had already made a visit to his apartment building. The police had uncovered his address and removed his personal belongings. He needed documents and a ticket out of New York. Then, he would have access to the money in his offshore account in the Cayman islands.

Stealthily making his way through the city, he stole the items necessary for his survival. Parked vehicles had been easy targets. By 12:00 noon he had taken money left in the glove compartments of the cars. It was time to return to the old building. He had taken too many chances already and his luck wouldn't hold up forever. He made his way back to the warehouse. Removing the plywood from the broken window, he slipped into his sanctuary. A rat scrambled for safety. Slowly, Emerald crept up the treacherous staircase and entered a room. The candles would provide some light. An old cot was lifted from its folded position and spread out near the wall. Emerald slumped onto it. The flickering light of the candle reflected images of old furniture. The warehouse had been used as a furniture depot at an earlier time. Now, the remaining building lay in ruins along with remnants of its past scattered throughout. Emerald wondered how long it had been vacated. He hoped it was not a refuge for the derelicts he'd seen earlier that day. To him they would only be trouble.

A wind howled outside the building and raindrops pelted the window. He gazed at a copy of the New York Times. It reported an all-points surveillance was under way. Lieutenant Brown had stated it was just a matter of time before the escapee would be back in custody. Emerald knew differently. He had been raised in the slums of New York. He knew the lay-out of the city better than anyone and would use it to his advantage.

The cot was uncomfortable, and throughout the night he adjusted himself on the metal frame. Its uneven coils nagged at his body. The more he thought of his miserable surroundings, the more he despised the cop who had taken him into custody. Emerald rested uneasy during the night, finally awaking to the scurrying sound of a rat. He reached for his shoe and hurled it at the intruder. The furry creature squeaked loudly, as the shoe made contact. The wounded animal dashed for a damaged wall and slithered from sight.

"If only I had a gun, they would show some respect," he mumbled. Emerald lifted himself onto the edge of the cot and glanced out from the grimy window. Light rain had fallen, its thin wet blanket covered the broken pavement. A shiver ascended his spine as the dampness penetrated his body. The street was now coming to life. Emerald combed back his thick greasy strands of hair. Paranoid feelings arose within him. Cautiously, he opened the door to the room and looked out. Assured no one was within the building, he crept down the staircase. Removing the plywood, he crawled through the opening. Two shabby figures hovered over a blazing fire rubbing their hands together. Emerald wanted no contact with them. He couldn't understand what possessed them to stand around all day doing nothing. In his mind, he believed they gave the city a bad reputation?

The core of New York was beginning to bustle with activity. He didn't think the cops would recognize him even if they were within arms distance. As two bohemians walked toward him, a feeling of repulsion passed though his mind. With them around he thought, New York wasn't a safe place. Emerald didn't think himself bigoted, he actually had talked to them on occasion. The way he saw it, the city would be better off with fewer of them. In the distance, he noticed an empty phone booth. Walking toward it, he entered, then closed the damaged door to afford himself some privacy. Emerald dropped a coin into the slot and dialled the number which had been stored in the memory centre of his brain. The number was his life line, it would provide him with survival. The phone continued to whale its ring. Impatient, he cursed under his breath. After minutes had passed, he slammed the phone back onto the receiver and wrenched opened the door.

After walking briskly for five minutes, Emerald Lee entered the small dilapidated building which housed Joe's Eatery. Music filtered through the greasy smoked filled atmosphere. A buxom blonde approached his table.

"What'll it be Mac?" she blurted out.

"My name isn't Mac! Don't they teach you any manners around here?" he asked.

"I was only trying to be friendly. I'm sorry if I offended you, what would you like?" she smiled.

"Chili and toast. Heavy on the peppers, I'm frozen stiff from all the rain," he replied. The waitress walked into the kitchen and yelled the order to the chef. His eyes studied her as she walked back to his table. Her bodacious curvature stretched at the buttoned uniform and her hips vibrated as she walked. The waitress placed a steaming cup of coffee on the clean table top.

"Compliments of the house. Sorry I offended you. You remind me of someone I've seen before." Emerald's heart raced. Was the disguise not working? Had she seen his picture in the Times?

"Yea, that's it. You look like the guy who sang in the sixties. You know the singer who died in the plane crash," she added.

"You got it all wrong. I've never been a singer and never been killed in a plane crash," he replied.

The waitress burst out laughing. She seemed a little slow but Emerald liked her anyway. She walked off and soon returned with a bowl of his favourite food. His stomach growled with hunger as he bolted down the steaming meal. His insides warming with each spoonful shoved into his mouth. He motioned the waitress over to his table.

"I'd like another cup of coffee. Do you have a phone I can use?" he asked. The waitress pointed toward the depth of the restaurant. Emerald walked to the phone and withdrew a coin from his pocket. Once again he dialled the number stored in his memory. Max would be his only chance. Finally after repeated rings, a familiar voice answered.

"Max it's me, Emerald!" he stated emphatically.

"Why are you calling me at home? They've got an APB out on you."

"You still owe me money for the last hit! I need it now!" said Lee.

"Don't get so touchy. I've got the cash for you. How did you get caught? I told you to get out after you hit your target."

"My timing was off. I didn't know the cops had the place staked out. Someone should have told me the target was under surveillance. Anyway, they don't know a thing about the operation. They've written me off as a psycho. I need my money, bring it to me tomorrow," Emerald described the meeting place.

"Yea I know the place," was the reply.

Emerald placed the phone back on the hook. Things were starting to look up for him. He walked back to the table and sat down. He picked up his cup and gulped down the thick savory beverage. He left the waitress a small tip as he got up from the table. She thanked him as he walked past her. The waitress asked if he would be back tomorrow. Emerald knew it wouldn't be a good idea to return. Someone could catch on to his identity. By tomorrow, he wouldn't need the coins in his pocket. His meeting with Max would change his financial status. Emerald Lee didn't like the idea of returning to the old building. A flashlight stolen from Macey's department store weighed down his pocket. It would be a good substitute for the candles. The thought of sleeping one more night in the damp rat infested room revolted him. Max would bring him the money. It would be his ticket out of New York.

The wind blew frigid gusts at him as he fought his way through the damp air. Just as he stepped from the curb, a middle-aged lady stepped into his path. The sullen face appeared familiar. He strained to get a second look. She was startled and looked up at Emerald. The frightened woman smiled hesitantly, her teeth protruding from puffy lips. She resembled Alice Holmes, the social worker from Bingham. Emerald believed Alice probably came to this section of the city to save a few souls. He would avoid contact with her.

An eerie silence hung in the air as he approached the deserted building. Emerald crawled through the hidden entrance and yanked the flashlight from his pocket. The beam of light was pointed into the bowels of the building. An animal brushed past his leg, he startled and let out an echoing yell. A howl emerged from the animal as he stepped on its tail. He called out to the cat as it scampered off into the darkness. If he could persuade the animal to return, it would afford some protection against the rats. The animal hesitated, but then cautiously approached and nuzzled its body against his leg. He wondered whether someone else was in the building? Emerald froze in his tracks and listened. Could a derelict have invaded his territory while he was out? He picked up the cat and quickly retreated to his room. Everything was in order, reassuring him no one had entered. Emerald closed the door and placed an old wardrobe against it. If someone tried to break in during the night, it would alert him and provide the minutes needed to prepare for an attack.

Emerald looked out at the deserted street through the stained window. In quiet reflection, he wondered whether the cat would do its job. The thought of rats climbing over him while he slept created a sense of revulsion. On many of his missions behind enemy lines, he'd been forced into dangerous positions but somehow having to hold up in a desolate, rat infested building forced the harsh reality of life at him.

During the night, he tossed constantly in his agitated state of sleep. A creaking sound awakened him from his light sleep. Raising his head, he looked across the room. Rats scurried into the far wall.

"Where is that damned cat?" he muttered. The animal was nowhere in sight. Emerald wondered how it could have gotten out. His fingers explored the area beneath the cot for his shoes. A furry animal brushed past his wrist. His hand retracted quickly from the unseen animal. Emerald peered over the side of the cot at the cavity beneath. The cat was resting against his shoes. Agitated by his lack of sleep, he sat on the side of the cot. Looking out through the window, he could see the penetrating rays of the sun beginning to creep through the structures on the opposite side of the street. Lifting himself from the cot, he made his way through the room. Opening the door, Emerald looked out to reassure himself no one had entered the warehouse during the night. He had an appointment with Max and made his way to the restaurant across the street. Emerald startled as someone called out to him. A shabby figure approached.

"Mister, have you seen my cat?" asked the old derelict.

"What does it look like?" inquired Emerald. The old man described the cat. As he turned to walk away, the derelict called out his name. Cautiously, Emerald walked toward the stranger.

"How do you like the disguise?" asked the derelict.

"You could have fooled me, thanks for coming Max. I knew my luck wouldn't hold up forever." Reaching down, Emerald took the brown canvas bag and glanced inside.

"Twenty-thousand! In ten and twenty dollar bills," said Max.

"I need another job Max. One that will bring enough cash to keep me out of the country for some time."

"Are you crazy? They've got an APB out on you. You're a wanted man. If they find out you're involved with our organization, we're finished. No one can find out about the operation!" he said emphatically.

"I can take care of myself. I've done a lot of jobs for the organization and I've never messed up before. This one was different. The businessman was being closely guarded. Someone should have told me he was under surveillance."

"Emerald, don't get so uptight. I'm just trying to do you a favour. You know how the organization works. I will talk to the commander. "Where can I reach you?"

"I can't be reached," was the reply.

"Okay have it your way, but take my cell phone. The number isn't traceable. I will contact you in a few days. You have to leave the city! Do you understand?" Emerald shoved the phone in his pocket. He knew it would be easier, now that he had the money. He looked up to thank his friend, but Max had already vanished. Emerald clutched the canvas bag under his arm as he walked toward the deserted building. He now had the means to escape from New York.

CHAPTER 17

Warm rays of the late afternoon sun shone into the small room removing the dampness which had crept in. Lack of activity had made him restless. Many unanswered questions passed through his mind. Emerald Lee wondered whether the authorities would be able to track him? It would be in his interest to lie low until the surveillance blew over. A copy of the New York Times lay on the floor by his cot. Emerald Lee reached down and retrieved it. The newspaper carried the story on the front page. He stared at the sketch, the picture depicted him well. The dye used to tint his hair and the newly grown moustache would provide him with some cover for now.

The sun was quickly sinking behind the tall building in the west. His room was growing darker. Dampness gripped his fingers as he fumbled with the thin laces on his shoes. It would be safe to leave the building. Few would notice him as they fought and elbowed their way through the rush hour traffic. New York possessed an anonymity which Emerald had always liked. No one could subject him to their microscopic analysis. He would avoid areas which could prove unfavourable. The diversion would cost him time, but it would ensure his safety. Street walkers dressed in their finest clothing passed him on the desolate street. They were wrapped up in their own thoughts and had little time for him.

He was almost in sight of the Army Surplus Store. Emerald recognized the restaurant where he first met her. It would take some persuasion to convince Brenda to leave New York. Emerald strained to get a look through the dripping condensation of the fogged window. Walking into the premise, he noticed a vacant booth near the rear wall. It would give him a vantage point, in case unknown enemies made their way through the door. A waitress walked over and asked for his order. She looked quizzically at him and glanced down at her order pad ready to act at his command.

"I'll have chili and toast, heavy on the peppers," he said. As he sat thinking over his plans, a young vivacious female hurried from the kitchen. Emerald instantly recognized her as she neared the table.

"Can I buy you a coffee?" he asked. Brenda startled as she turned toward him.

"I just finished my shift and have to get something," she said.

"Have you ordered yet?" Emerald nodded.

"Eat your meal and I'll return soon." Brenda pushed the door open and made her way out to the sidewalk. A waitress approached and placed the steaming bowl in front of him. The chili was not as spicy as he liked it. He was irritated things changed so quickly. The pages of the Times were turned rapidly in succession. He could not find anything about his case. Just as he gulped his last drop of coffee, Brenda entered. She walked over to his table and sat in the chair facing him.

"Tell me you didn't have nothing to do with that killing. I've been reading the Times. I just can't believe you are the same person they described in the paper. You told me you were a computer analyst and travelled on assignment. Let's get out of here before someone puts something together. You have a lot of explaining," she added. Emerald placed the twenty dollar bill on the table. They left before the waitress could return. He tugged at the zipper of his jacket, as they stepped outside.

"It sure is damp for this time of year," he said.

"Yea, I know what you mean. I hate this wet weather. It's not much further from here," she added.

They continued for another block, then entered the low rise apartment building.

"I moved in two weeks ago. After the story hit the press, I didn't want the authorities paying me a visit. If they found out about us, it would cause one big headache for me," she stated. They walked up the staircase and entered her apartment.

"Make yourself a coffee. You'll find everything you need above the stove." Brenda excused herself and walked to the bathroom. He could hear the shower rumbling behind the closed door. Emerald felt grimy, he hadn't taken a shower since his escape from the hospital. Plugging the kettle into the electrical socket, he glanced at the items in the cupboard. The instant coffee was removed from the middle shelf. As he waited, Emerald nosed through the apartment. She did not have any of his pictures on the wall. Brenda had learned to play the game well. He knew she was looking after his best interests. In the background, he could hear the kettle whistling. Grabbing it with his left hand, he poured hot water over the brown coffee crystals. With his beverage in hand, he walked into the living room and sat on the sofa. A few minutes passed, then Brenda entered the room dressed in a bathrobe.

"We are going to stay here this evening."

"Sounds like a good idea," Emerald replied. Brenda walked to the stereo and flicked the switch.

"That's my favourite station!" he added.

"Yes I know, now tell me the truth Emerald! What happened," she asked.

"First, I would like to take a shower". Brenda led him to the washroom. A clean towel was withdrawn from the closet. Removing his clothes, he could sense the foul smell of his body.

"Would you dig out some of my clothes Brenda? You can throw these ones in the garbage." Emerald knew a shower would be needed to remove the pungent smell of sweat. As he stood under the shower head, Emerald imagined the filth from his body swirling into the drain. Finishing the ordeal, he stepped onto the bath mat and towelled his body. Retrieving the clothes from the rack, he quickly dressed. Emerald walked into the living room and seated himself on the sofa next to Brenda. He studied her profile as he sensed her aromatic perfume drifting toward him. Emerald nudged toward her and buried his lips onto the nape of her neck. Brenda giggled and pressed herself into him, allowing Emerald to explore her. As his hand wandered through the semi-opened bathrobe, Brenda sighed. Her light touch caressed his firmly muscled chest and then wandered down toward his stomach. Emerald could sense his sexual energy. Moving his face from her breast, he slid closely toward her.

"I really missed you," she said gasping. Brenda pulled him toward her and his weight was absorbed into the roundness of her body.

CHAPTER 18

Emerald rolled over to Brenda's side of the bed, but she was gone. He lifted himself as Brenda appeared at the doorway.

"You were tired, you slept for 10 hours. This will wake you! Help yourself to breakfast. There is plenty to eat in the fridge. I'll see you later," she said. Brenda placed a cup of coffee on the night table, bent over and kissed him. She hurried from the room and the door closed behind her. Drinking the warm beverage, Emerald reflected on his predicament. He raised himself from the bed and walked toward the kitchen. A second cup of coffee would help him collect his thoughts. He thought back to the conversation with Max Winters. If Max could persuade them, they would give him one more assignment and then he would have the money to leave New York for good. He wouldn't tell them his plan but would disappear with Brenda. It would be better this way.

Emerald gulped down the coffee and left the apartment. The coolness of the morning air caressed his body causing him to shiver. He wondered whether it was fear or the dampness in the air. In the distance, he could see people scurrying into the subway tunnel. Emerald sprinted for the staircase. It would be faster this way. Tension raced through his body, Emerald wondered whether he could trust Brenda. The subway train slowed and the door swung open. As he walked toward the rear of the compartment, terror gripped him. Emerald noticed a young cop sitting on the left-hand side of the car. Two eyes riveted on him as he moved to the back. Sliding onto a seat, he watched the suspicious cop from the corner of his eye. The cop turned and looked in his direction. Emerald stared intently at the newspaper, partially covering his face. He wasn't sure if he had been recognized. To spring from his seat, would only alert the officer. He waited, eyeing his would-be captor through his peripheral vision. The chance finally came. A fat lady loaded down with parcels approached the rear exit. Just as she got there, he quickly elbowed his way in front of her. She glared at him in a menacing way. The train stopped and Emerald sprung forward. The obese woman slowed the cop, allowing him to escape. Moving forward, he glanced back and could see the cop in pursuit. Gripped by fear, Emerald sprinted like a jackal.

"Stop that man!" yelled the cop. Looking back, Emerald could see the uniformed figure pursuing him with gun in hand. He no longer dodged bystanders, but bowled them over in his attempt to escape. An open alley appeared on his right. He veered into it, the cop followed twenty yards behind.

"Stop or I'll shoot!" echoed the voice behind, as he darted for the open warehouse. Two quick shots rang out as Emerald dove for the doorway. The whistling bullets smashed into the brick wall where he had been only seconds before. He rolled behind some crates. In desperation, he sprung to his feet and moved for cover at the rear of the warehouse. He could hear footsteps approaching the entrance of the building.

"I know you're in there. Give up now and come out with your hands high. I'm giving you two minutes," said the cop. Emerald breathed heavily. He cleared the sweat from his brow. He wasn't going down this way. The cop made his move, footsteps inched toward the crates. Emerald moved back quietly, hoping not to alert the officer. A shadow on the far wall reflected the ominous figure with gun withdrawn. Emerald moved deeper into the warehouse.

"Okay, don't move. I've got you covered. One step and you're a dead man," shouted the cop. Emerald froze in his tracks. He was ready to stand when he decided instead to peer out from his lair. It was a bluff, the cop was facing the opposite side of the warehouse. Emerald made his move. With the cunning of a fox, he inched toward his opponent. He picked up a claw-bar from the floor beside one of the empty crates. When he was within striking distance, he sprang to his feet. The cop turned with the Glock special in hand. The weight of the swinging bar smashed at the gun. A shot rang out and the weapon tumbled to the grimy floor. As the cop dove for the gun, Emerald's foot made contact with the man's jaw. A loud crack echoed through the building. The uniformed man jerked backward. Emerald's heel delivered a second blow. The cop went down. Emerald aggressively wielded the claw-bar above his head and was about to deliver the blow which would cease the man's life. A throbbing feeling deep in his right temple, gripped at him. At first, it was barely noticeable, then it ached with the intensity of a migraine. Emerald Lee looked down at the blood oozing from the cop's open wound, then something triggered a sense of anxiety and panic deep inside his brain. He felt nauseous and threw down the metal bar. Cautiously, he retrieved the handgun. Emerald bent forward and felt the wrist of his fallen victim. Life still pulsed through the man's veins. In his profession, he had been paid to hit targets. His motto had always been, two extra bullets into his downed victim. This one was different, something inside told him the cop was an innocent victim. Emerald Lee did not like the way he felt. Dizzy and sick to his stomach, he vomited. Slowly, he withdrew from the unconscious man. As he wiped the sweat from his forehead, he wondered whether he had contracted a virus. Creeping forward, he slowly opened the door and looked out at the bystanders collected at the front entrance. Without hesitation, he ran to the opposite side of the building and left through a side entrance. He would have to avoid detection. A tall metal fence obstructed his escape from the alley. Emerald leaped onto the wire mesh and bounded over. Leaving the alley, caution would be needed if he was going to make it back to his lair.

Detective Brown was notified and on the scene within twenty minutes. He inquired about witnesses. The investigating officer brought forward a short fat man.

"This man saw the whole thing! Tell Lieutenant Brown what you saw," said the cop. The detective listened carefully as the short, fat Italian recreated the event. The police officer had chased a medium built suspect. As the fleeing man dodged into the warehouse, the cop fired. Mr. Lugani recalled at that point, he ran to his shop and telephoned the police.

"How long were they in the warehouse, Mr. Lugani?"

The short, balding man scratched his head. "It must have been at least fifteen minutes. It took me about five minutes to reach my shop, make the call and then return. There was no one in sight by the time I got back."

Lieutenant Brown turned to the investigating officer. "What the hell took you guys so long?" The officer hesitated for a minute, then complained about the heavy traffic.

"Traffic, my ass," grumbled Brown.

"You said the suspect was of medium build. Do you think you could recognize him, if I showed you some pictures?" asked Detective Brown. Mr. Lugani nodded. Lieutenant Brown reached into his suit pocket and pulled out four snapshots. Mr. Lugani was asked to study them carefully. He was asked if any of the photos resembled the suspect. The short fat man puzzled over two of the pictures.

"Both of these pictures look like the guy I saw," he said. He carefully inspected the pictures.

"This is him, but there is something different. That's it, the guy I saw looked like this one, but his hair was greased down, he had a mustache and wore dark-rimmed glasses," said the grocer.

"Are you sure?" asked Lieutenant Brown.

"I'm positive," Mr. Lugani replied.

Lieutenant Brown took the pictures and tucked them back into the inside pocket of his suit jacket. The witness had identified Emerald Lee. The rookie from the Bronx had been busted up pretty badly. Lieutenant Brown wondered what had prevented Lee from killing the cop. The suspect probably thought the cop was dead when he left. Lieutenant Brown knew psychopathic killers rarely let their victims live. He thought back to his days in the Gulf War. When the enemy was down, you finished him. To let him live would only be asking for trouble. He believed Emerald thought the same way. The detective wondered why Emerald had come to this section of town? He would search every inch of the district. Someone must have seen him leave. There had to be some leads. No one could vanish into thin air. He jumped into the cruiser and radioed the precinct dispatcher.

"This is Lieutenant Brown calling. Contact all units and send every available man to the corner of 51st and Second Avenue. I have an eyewitness description of the suspect Emerald Lee. Send down our sketch artist," Brown signed off.

"Mr. Lugani our artist is going to be here soon. I'll bring him over to your shop as soon as he arrives. Constable Henry get on the radio and tell all units the suspect is armed and dangerous. He is to be shot on sight if he tries to escape." Lieutenant Brown walked over to the warehouse. He inspected the area where the officer had fallen. A claw-bar lay nearby. He took out his handkerchief and picked up the weapon. Emerald had probably used it on his victim. He would send it to the Forensic lab for evaluation. There would likely be finger prints and traces of the downed officer's blood. Lieutenant Brown walked from the building. The police artist was getting out of a cruiser.

"Hello Frank, good to see you could make it. We have a lead on the maniac who escaped from Bingham. Our witness, Mr. Lugani thinks he can describe him to you. Come on, let's go talk to him." They walked over to the corner shop. Mr. Lugani was still wringing his hands from the excitement. He had always wanted to get his name in the paper. Perhaps this would be his big chance. The short corpulent man knew he could describe the suspect with his eyes closed.

"Mr. Lugani, this is Constable Frank Horner our artist," said Brown. The two men shook hands. Lieutenant Brown produced the photograph of Emerald Lee. Constable Horner went to work sketching in the details the grocer described.

"Okay, give me some greased down hair, a mustache and some dark-rimmed glasses," said Lieutenant Brown.

"It's perfect!" shouted Mr. Lugani as he jumped up and down excitedly.

"That's him without a doubt, or my name isn't Francesco Giovanni Lugani."

"Are you one hundred percent sure, Mr. Lugani?"

"Believea me, that's a him," said the grocer no longer attempting to hide his heavy Italian accent.

They thanked the short man for his assistance and left the store. Mr. Lugani was excited with his new found celebrity status. He would buy the evening edition of the newspaper. His name would be in the Times, and on the television evening news. He hoped the article would spell his name correctly. His relatives in Italy would be proud. His parents would talk of their son for months.

"Frank, would you make another sketch for me and then get your copy to our Printer. Have him circulate copies to all precincts immediately. Get a copy to the Times. I want it in the evening edition. I want our boy caught within 48 hours. He's not getting away this time," said Brown. Constable Horner quickly sketched a second copy of the suspect and handed it to Lieutenant Brown. He left the building and jumped into the cruiser. The tires squealed as the car sped off. Uniformed officers were swarming over the area.

"Sergeant, get those men over here now," shouted Lieutenant Brown.

"Officers, I'm Lieutenant Brown from Precinct 14. Our most wanted criminal was in this area during the last hour. He put one of New York's finest in intensive care. He's evaded us for the last week. Now, we have him in our palms. To the man who gets him,

I'll guarantee a commendation from our mayor. I have a sketched picture of him, study it well. As soon as you've looked it over, I want you to move out and each take a block. Get any information you can. Remember, he's armed and dangerous. Take due caution and shoot him on sight," said the detective. Lieutenant Brown loosened his tie and walked over to his car. He was going to personally take part in the search. He wanted to be on the scene when Emerald Lee was taken. Lieutenant Brown would be there to make sure the job was done properly this time.

CHAPTER 19

A northeasterly wind howled while Emerald Lee read and re-read the old edition of the Times. He paced the floor as he stared out through the grimy window. Few had passed and no one had even glanced at the building. The gun was loaded and lay beside the cot. If anyone attempted to get to him, he would be ready. Dusk was approaching and the overcast skies were in his favour. It would be safe to leave his den as soon as darkness set over the city. Placing a black toque over his head and slipping on his jacket, he made his way down the stairs. The air was cold and the wind piercing as he crawled out from the building. With the black toque pulled down, his identity would be secure. Emerald cautiously looked in all directions as he walked quickly through the empty streets. He approached the newspaper box and dropped four coins into the slot. The front page of the paper carried a full article of his attack on the officer. Reading the report, he was irritated by the way the press had distorted the story. It almost appeared as if he had stalked the cop. He wondered how they obtained the sketch. As he read further, he was relieved the cop hadn't died.

Sprinting across the street, he entered the phone booth. He had to get a message to Brenda. Depositing a coin, Emerald dialled her home number. As he waited, a police cruiser slowly drove past. The vehicle proceeded down the street and stopped in front of a restaurant. A tall officer got out, then walked into the building. Emerald breathed a sigh of relief. It almost appeared as though they were closing in on him. His paranoia was beginning to take over, he would have to get out of New York. A faint voice answered at the other end.

"Brenda, this is Emerald. I'm on my way over. Just thought I'd call first to check if you were home, see you soon." As he hung up the phone, he wondered why she did not sound the same. He didn't think she would turn him in, but there was always a possibility Detective Brown had discovered her identity and set the trap. Detective Brown had made a statement in the media, something to the effect the perpetrator would be in lockup in forty eight hours. Had the trap been set and Brenda the bait? He had to think it over before going to her place. He didn't want to go down this way. Emerald had known Brenda for two years. When he first met her at the restaurant, Emerald mentioned he was a computer programmer. His job frequently took him out of town. She had never questioned his work nor appeared suspicious. The situation had now changed. He was a wanted man and new charges were being added to the list every day as he remained at large. The last time he was at Brenda's apartment, she was receptive. Emerald wondered whether he could still trust her?

Pedestrian traffic was heavy as he neared the central core of Manhattan. He knew the police would be looking for him. They would be searching for a man with glasses and slicked down hair. He hurried into a bus depot and descended the stairs to the washroom. A navy blue trench coat hung near the sink. He could see the feet of the occupant in the stall. Grabbing the trench coat, he bounded up the stairs then pushed through the double doors leading to the street. The coat was a little on the large side but would serve the purpose. He had cut his hair with the scissors found in the deserted warehouse. His new disguise would protect him for now. He entered the tunnel entrance and waited for the subway train to reach the platform. A paranoia overcame him. Would a cop be waiting to follow him? He looked downward at the floor as he moved cautiously to the rear of the coach. He watched the signs on the tunnel wall as the train sped along the tracks toward Bridge Station. The subway train came to a stop. He filed off with the other passengers, shuffling forward as they made their way from the tunnel.

A calmness filtered through the evening air, like the quiet before the storm. The apartment building was now in sight. As he approached it, Emerald stared at a blue van parked across the street from her apartment. Inside the vehicle he could hear movement. Expecting to see officers lunge out at him, Emerald gripped at the Glock handgun in his pocket. Cautiously, he peered into the vehicle but could only see two dogs wrestling on the carpeted floor.

Emerald approached her apartment building and entered. A faint melodic tune floated into the hallway. He recognized it as a song from an earlier time when life was idyllic. Emerald bounded up the staircase, but at each floor level expected to see someone charge out at him. On the third floor, he turned to his right and knocked. Brenda opened the door and looked nervously in his direction. Emerald entered the apartment.

"Where are they?" he nervously blurted out.

"Where are who?" she said.

"Oh, I thought your friends were coming over for a drink," he replied.

"I don't remember telling you that."

"I guess I must have been dreaming this morning," he responded. Brenda left the room and returned with a bottle of whisky.

"You're a little edgy, I think you need this," she said. Emerald examined the bottle then poured two drinks, handing one to Brenda. She started talking about her day at work, then abruptly stopped in mid-sentence. "I saw the paper! Are you the one who laid out the cop?" she asked.

"I was on my way to retrieve the money. The officer noticed me on the train and came after me. I didn't want anything to do with him and couldn't believe it when he started shooting at me.

I hit him in self-defense, but I didn't try to kill him as they stated in the paper. If I wanted to kill him, I could have finished him in the warehouse."

"The police came to the restaurant. They were asking all sorts of questions"?

"What did you tell them Brenda?" he asked inquisitively.

"I mentioned a lot of people came here. I told them I didn't see no one fitting your description. I don't think they have us connected," she said. He sipped his drink and looked at her. She appeared almost too apprehensive. They talked for a short time and then Brenda walked into the bedroom. Emerald followed and lay beside her. Brenda snuggled up to him and caressed his chest. Deep in thought, he did not respond.

"Don't you want to get romantic?" she asked.

"I have a lot of things on my mind Brenda. How about later?" Frustrated, Brenda rolled over to her side of the bed. Emerald reflected on better times. He would have to call Max in the morning, the time had come to leave New York.

CHAPTER 20

Emerald awoke and lifted himself from the comfort of the bed. Brenda lay beside him in a deep sleep. Rather than disturb her, he quietly crept from the warm sheets. Grabbing the bathrobe from the top of the dresser, he made his way to the kitchen. Plugging in the kettle, Emerald noticed a copy of the Times on the table. Staring at the article, he slowly read it. The sketch of him looked good. Lieutenant Brown had personally commented on the intensive manhunt.

"What type of guru does he think he is?" muttered Emerald. The kettle howled in the background. He unplugged it and dumped two teaspoons of instant coffee into a cup and splashed hot water over the crystals. Brenda was stirring in the bedroom, he walked in and smiled at her.

"Would you like a coffee?" he asked.

"Sure, I'll be right there, but first I'd like to take a shower," she smiled. As Brenda lifted herself from the bed, Emerald inspected her slender frame. She walked to the bathroom. He could hear the shower droning in the background. A brief silence prevailed, then she entered the kitchen fully dressed. Brenda reached for the cup of coffee and gulped down the beverage.

"I've got to get to work, see you later," she said as she bolted through the door. He was now alone and would make the call. The number was stored in his mind, ready to be accessed at any time. Emerald thought back to the first time he met his associate. Max had approached him in a bar. After a few beer, they talked of their battle experiences. Max had also experienced poverty in the slums of New York. Hand to hand military combat was similar to their early years in the neighbourhood. A strong bond formed between the soldiers as they adapted to war on the front lines. It was after a mission deep into enemy territory, both had been wounded. After spending three months in an American hospital, they received honourable discharges and were sent back to the States.

At first, New York was exciting. But after returning to the drudgery of a nine to five job, both men had come to despise the lifestyle of the ordinary man. Finally their break came. A friend had returned from the mid-East. He had been fighting as a mercenary. Max Winters was able to persuade the man to get them a contract. With the skills acquired in battle, Emerald and Max were assigned positions as mercenary soldiers in the mid-East. During a brief stint in Iraq, they had made contact with the commander of the European Liberation Order. His purpose for travelling to the Iraqi front was to recruit mercenaries for his cause. He quickly persuaded them to quit the militia ranks for greater rewards. They would be trained to use more lethal techniques. Emerald displayed the personality necessary for the task. He cared little for others and was impulsive. He relished employment which would stimulate his mind and put his skills into action.

The mercenaries would never meet the men who fronted the operation. It was rumoured a European businessman was the mastermind behind the organization. He obtained the contracts and assigned them to his soldiers. Max Winters quickly rose to power in the organization. He was now leading the American Liberation Order, a terrorist group hostile to the United States. Emerald had faltered on his last operation, it would take some time before they would trust him again. Now he needed Max. He wondered whether his friend would be ready to bail him out?

Emerald picked up the phone. He hesitated for a brief moment, and then dialled the number. A light perspiration surfaced on his brow as the phone continued ringing. Finally, the audible click confirmed contact.

"Max, it's Emerald! Can we talk?"

"Yea, we can but I have to tell you the people at the top are a little concerned about you. They weren't happy with the last job. They told me if this one doesn't pan out, you're finished. You know what that means?" he said. A pause followed as Emerald cleared his throat.

"I understand what you're saying." Emerald knew when a mercenary was kicked out of the organization, no questions were asked. He would be their next target. Someone would come for him, that was the way the European Liberation Order operated.

"I won't fail again Max."

"Okay, I know you won't screw up. I'll see you this afternoon at two o'clock. Same place as last time." Emerald agreed to be there. He would get his chance, this would be the final operation. With the money in his offshore account, he and Brenda would live in seclusion in the Caribbean. The final job would give him the necessary leverage. It would provide him with the time to put his plan into action. Subconsciously, he knew it was just a matter of time before they sent their hired assassins to terminate him.

Emerald quickly dressed and left the apartment. He would return to the old building. Money would be needed to buy a new identity. With the proper documents, he could leave the country. Pushing his way through the crowded street, he did not look at the people gathered at the subway entrance. It was always packed at rush hour. His new haven in the Caribbean would be different. They would have a more relaxed life. As he looked up, he could see the train approaching. Emerald shuffled into the car with the others. A quick glance at the subway map indicated there were only four stops until he arrived at his destination.

Walking from the subway tunnel, Emerald recognized the familiar stench he'd known as a kid. He gagged as the foul smell penetrated his nostrils. Attempting to hold his breath, he walked quickly past the transients cluttered at the edges of the street. Like hungry lost animals, they eyed him. When he was beyond the area, Emerald breathed deeply. He could feel the fresh air move downward into his lungs. More transients shuffled past him as he walked in the direction of the old warehouse. Their hungry stares caused a sense of discomfort. From the corner of his eye, he watched. They could never be trusted. Like hungry jackals, they would spring upon any unsuspecting victim. He had known the violence of a transient once before. Emerald thought back to a disturbing period of his life. His mother had been arguing with her boyfriend. They had retreated to the bedroom as he sat watching television in the cold, empty living room. The haunting sounds still penetrated the conscious recess of his mind. He attempted to repress the memory of the event. There had been a loud violent argument. Hurrying to the bedroom door, he squinted to get a look through the keyhole. Almost immediately, the door swung open. The large foul smelling man grabbed him by the throat. Emerald fought desperately to escape the hold which was slowly squeezing the life from his body. He bit the man's hand fiercely drawing blood. The hold was released. As Emerald dropped to the floor, a whisky bottle smashed against his skull, he slipped into unconsciousness. His finger slowly traced the scar on his face which extended from his forehead down to his temple. He fought to repress the thought of his bad childhood.

Cautiously circling the building, Emerald entered by a broken window. Only the wind howling through the cracked window panes penetrated the silence of the deserted structure. Loose planks were removed from the floor and the canvas bag taken from the dark recess. Five thousand dollars was counted from the bundle and shoved into the pockets of his trench coat. Emerald suspiciously eyed the room, then shoved the bag into the recess. He re-positioned the wooden planks. In a half-hour, Max would meet him and provide him with the plans. Then, he would make the necessary contacts. The forged documents would be expensive, but would allow him an escape hatch. He withdrew Brenda's picture from his pocket. The new passports would allow them to leave New York.

Emerald looked at the cracked crystal of his watch. He would hurry to the meeting place. Max didn't like to be kept waiting. Cautiously, he picked his way between the buildings and down the alleyway. He couldn't take the chance of being followed. Arriving at the meeting place, he edged himself between the two buildings. As he rubbed his hands together, the black limousine pulled up to the curb. The driver rolled down the window and looked out at him. He motioned Emerald to get into the vehicle.

"Good to see you," said the dark occupant.

"I appreciate everything you've done Max."

"Just don't screw this one up. The captain contacted me last week. The cops had been following him. He slipped away and a boat took him out of the country two days ago. Contacts were made while he was in Canada. You're leaving New York tonight, your destination is Toronto. They'll probably be watching the airports. Your best bet is the train to Boston and then a flight to Toronto. Someone will meet you at the Pearson International airport on Saturday at eight in Terminal Three. You're to wear this insignia on the lapel of your jacket. They'll fill you in on the details. I will deposit twenty thousand in your Cayman account now and the other half when the job is finished. Are there any questions?" he asked. Emerald shook his head. He thanked his associate and stepped from the car. In the morning, he would leave for Boston and from there take a flight to Toronto.

CHAPTER 21

Emerald Lee looked out from the AC-10 quickly approaching the runway. Lights blinked upward
from the city below. Music piped in through the headset was replaced by the melodic voice of the stewardess informing passengers the plane was about to land. Snapping his buckle shut, he attempted to look out from the porthole window blurred by condensation. Tires of the AC-10 screeched upon impact.

Emerald thought back to the times he had been dropped behind enemy lines. Once more he would experience the taste of battle. The plane vibrated as the pilot applied the airbrakes. He sensed the deceleration as it quickly came to a halt. A tight sensation worked its way up from his stomach, through his chest and into his throat. He could feel the pressure in his inner ear as he rolled his jaw. Finally his ears popped, relieving the tension in his head. Looking over at the older couple beside him, he could see the expression of terror in their faces. A sense of pleasure passed through his mind. But as quickly as the thought occurred, he experienced a feeling of nausea and apprehension. A sharp pain radiated in his right temple. When he completed this mission, Emerald would seek medical consultation. Ever since his stay at Bingham hospital, his health seemed to be deteriorating. He wondered whether the doctors had successfully removed the haemorrhage from his brain?

Leaving the aircraft, a familiar line was uttered by the attractive attendant. He wondered why people were always trying so hard to be nice? His pace quickened across the tarmac and into the terminal building. From the directions he'd been given, the restaurant was on the upper level. But first, he would have to clear customs. He withdrew the small insignia from his pocket and attached it to his lapel as Max had directed him. From his pocket, he tugged at the passport which had cost him three grand. A mild sense of anxiety surfaced but quickly faded from his mind. He knew the forgery was a good one. With the newly grown beard and dyed hair, he would pass inspection. Emerald handed the customs officer the document.

"Business in Canada Sir?"

"No, pleasure! I'm here to visit some friends."

"Okay everything is in order! Have a good day," said the customs agent.

The money had been well spent. Emerald was travelling as Robert B. Williams. His papers had been well documented and authentic in appearance. Approaching the attendant at the car rental booth, he asked for directions to the restaurant. A smiling blonde woman pointed to the stairs and mentioned he had to turn to his right. Staccatoed voices filtered into the hallway as he opened the door. Cautiously, he glanced through the room and then walked toward an empty table in the corner. A waitress approached and placed a cup in front of him, filing it with coffee. Emerald glanced up and acknowledged her action. Five minutes passed as he sipped at the bitter sweet liquid. The same waitress approached and asked if he wanted another. Emerald shook his head. She looked at him intently and mouthed a message.

"Your friend said not to bother waiting here. He'll talk to you at the front of the restaurant," she smiled. Emerald thanked her as he placed a ten dollar bill on her tray. He walked toward the washroom and entered. Standing in front of the mirror, he studied his reflection and then combed his hair. He did not stay long but left the washroom and then walked toward the exit door. As he glanced down at his newspaper, two men walked from the washroom. Emerald eyed them briefly and then looked away. To stare too long could lead to an unwanted invitation. He didn't notice the figure exit from the washroom behind him. The man bumped into Emerald and glanced down at his insignia. He motioned Emerald to follow. A brief introduction was made outside the restaurant. His contact led him to a waiting car at the entrance to the terminal building. A door was opened and Emerald got in.

"Drive Al," said the man in the front seat. Car tires spun on the wet pavement. The robust passenger in the front seat turned and faced Emerald.

"There's been a leak in the operation. The captain was followed into Canada. He thought he lost them in Montreal. It looks like the RCMP know something about the operation. They arrested Tom, our explosives expert. We don't have to worry about him talking, he's been in rougher spots before. We have to move this operation ahead of schedule," said the commander. The car entered the expressway and headed west. A sign indicated they were now on the 401. City lights flickered behind them in the distance.

"Where are we going?" asked Emerald.

"We have a farmhouse near Guelph, not too far from here. I'd like to go over the plans tonight, as soon as everybody arrives. But first, I'd like to know what happened on your last assignment?" asked the commander.

"Somebody should have told me they had surveillance on Milano. No one knew we were going for him. Somebody let the cat out of the bag," said Emerald.

"What are you talking about? How could they have known he was our target? He was just a random hit, merely a decoy, so was his brother-in-law Richardson. They had nothing to do with this operation. Their only link was Dr. Jobin. He got cold feet and was going to inform the authorities. He took a bullet because of his betrayal. When the RCMP found out about the operation, we went after Richardson and Milano just to throw them off. We didn't think there would be surveillance on Milano. We wanted them to think this was about the Panax Corporation. Let's hope they are on a similar wavelength, and maintaining surveillance on Richardson. It will give us the extra days to complete this operation. By the time they put the whole thing together, we will be out of the country," said the commander.

"After they captured me they shipped me to the Clinton Correctional Facility. They told me I needed an operation and sent me to the Bingham Neurosurgical Centre. I'm convinced, the hospital was built for madmen. You should have seen the zombies in that place. Can you imagine a sane guy like me locked up with all those nuts?" asked Emerald.

"Don't worry Emerald, we know your not insane, your just a crazy psycho," blurted the commander. The driver and the commander burst out laughing. Emerald did not laugh.

"We are going to hook up with our contact in a few days. He's got the plans worked out and after that we should be reaping the rewards. This operation is all about money. We just have to convince the military we are terrorists. Once they realize we have the missiles, they should be willing to cooperate. Arrangements have been made, tomorrow we fly out. Monday is the test day, the exchange has to be done by Sunday. After that its simple, just execute the launch," said the commander.

"What are we hitting?" asked Emerald.

"All in due time my boy. Remember, in our line of work, nobody asks questions. The computer analyst will explain how to use the jamming device so the military can't re-route the missiles," said the commander. The vehicle slowed as they left the ramp and headed north. They were now driving along a country road. The car made a right turn into a driveway. A quarter mile up the gravel road, the vehicle was parked in front of the building. The commander got out of the car and opened the large door to the barn. The vehicle was driven inside, and the door closed.

"Precautions," smiled the commander. Emerald followed the aging commander into the house.

"Steve we're here!" yelled the commander.

"Be right down!" shouted the distant voice.

"Have a seat Emerald, I'll put the coffee on," said the commander. Emerald sunk onto a kitchen chair. He reflected on the events of the past week. He had escaped but still experienced massive migraines in his right temple. He wouldn't mention it to the others. No one liked a whiner and complainer. He would continue taking the pain killers Brenda had given him. With time, his headaches would likely go away.

"Are you still good with electronics Emerald?" asked the commander. "You name the job, and I can do it," said Emerald. As he sat drinking his coffee, Emerald watched cautiously as a tall thin man entered the room. From the scar on the man's forehead, Emerald realized the wound had recently been inflicted. As Emerald continued his stare, the man pointed at the scar.

"I bet you wonder how I got this? I was hit by shrapnel on our last assignment. The Swiss medical team told me they had done their best. From the scar left on my face I sorta don't believe them. After this one is over, I intend on having the job done right. There's a plastic surgeon in the Bahamas. He's got a good reputation and guarantees his work. He'd better do the job right or I'll reward him with a little lead therapy," Steve said with a smile.

Maps were spread over the table. The commander pointed to the area in Northwestern Alberta. He traced the route the aircraft would fly. The mercenaries would intercept the cargo plane at the military base in Cold Lake. By the time the officials were notified, the mercenaries would have made their escape. Systematically the commander drilled them on the plans. The details were important, if someone screwed up, the operation would fail. The conversation was abruptly interrupted by the ring of the telephone. The commander answered in a gruff voice.

"Where the hell are you? How long have they been following you? You've got to do something with the documents. Put them in a locker at Union station. What number? Okay, now get out of there as fast as you can." The commander slammed down the phone.

"That was Hans. He was able to dodge them but is holding up in Union station. You guys hang in here. I will retrieve him and the documents. Contact has been made with the major. We will carry out the operative as planned," he added. The commander put on his khaki jacket. As he exited the farmhouse, he thought back to the days in the commando division. Many of his men had gone down during that period. When they were down you left them. If they were wounded, you finished them. To leave a wounded man could bring torture at the hands of the enemy. This one was different, he couldn't leave his son behind enemy lines. He would retrieve the documents from the locker, then would go for his son.

CHAPTER 22

Sergeant James scratched his head as he looked over the evidence. The police had slipped up, and let the suspect get away. He wondered if there was a leak in the operation. He glanced over at his partner. "I can't believe we've got those idiots working for us."

"What now?" asked Sergeant Cormick.

"I don't know Ralph, everyone seems to have screwed up on this case. Our New York contingent let Emerald Lee get away. We had the mercenary under surveillance and he got out. The only person in custody is the electronics expert. He's not talking, only gives his rank and serial number. We ought to have the right to pry the information out of him, but this is North America. We can only use interrogation techniques advocated by the agency. I'm not sure what to do now. We are going to have to wait for their demands," said Sergeant James.

"A whole month's work down the pipes," replied Sergeant Cormick. Frank James realized the case was slowly collapsing around them. There had to be some angle they were missing. He had worked on this one for weeks but something just didn't wash. He thought about the men assigned to the case, but could only question the loyalty of two members. He wondered whether the undercover cops had sold out to the enemy. He would not share the information with Sergeant Cormick but go directly to his commanding officer. Maybe they could get a wire tap? It wouldn't be the first time one of their men had been bought.

"Let's go inspect the place they were using to head up their operation. Maybe something will turn up. There has to be some clue," said Sergeant James.

"I think the Forensic Unit combed the place," replied Sergeant Cormick.

"You never know what they might have overlooked. The Forensic squad is only as good as the people who do the analysis. Maybe they were sleeping on the job when they went through the place," he added. Forest Hill was not far from the station. Ten minutes passed as the two cops rode the distance in silence. A left turn was made and the car stopped at the stately stone clad home.

"At least they had good taste. This must have cost them a bundle," said Sergeant James.

"They were leasing this home. It turns out, a wealthy businessman from the Bahamas owns this place. According to the investigating officers, the owner is clean. They checked him out. He has nothing to do with this operation. He owns many places throughout the country and rents them out to high end executives. The mercenaries paid $5,000 dollars monthly for this place," replied Sergeant Cormick.

The vehicle was parked and the detectives walked over to the unmarked police car. Detective James flashed his badge at the on duty cop. "Anyone around this evening?" he asked.

"No! Nothing been moving since I came on shift," barked the overweight constable.

"We're going to check out a few things. If something comes up radio us," stated Sergeant James.

"Yep sure will," said the constable. They walked up to the house and let themselves into the residence. Ralph flipped the light switch.

"You keep an eye on things out here Ralph, I'm going to take a look around." Sergeant James moved quietly up the staircase.

Subconsciously, he knew no one was present, but his instincts and training prevailed. Caution had paid off in other situations. It would be wise to continue the practise. The house had been vacated in a hurry. Sergeant James wondered how they had gotten out so quickly. Someone must have warned them. There had to be a leak somewhere in Cormick's department. Someone must have gotten the information to them. He would have Ralph dig into the files of those assigned to the case. The terrorists had emptied the place before they left. Usually, there was a discarded cigarette butt but this operation was different. Not a shred of evidence had been found by the Forensic Unit. He checked each room and then left the second floor returning to the area below.

"Anything?" asked Sergeant Cormick.

"Nothing! I'm going to check out this floor and then I'm going into the basement. Keep an eye out and try to think like the suspects. There has to be something." He searched each room on the main floor and then made his way to the basement. A dampness pervaded the lower area of the house. Sergeant James examined every room and then entered the recreation room. Everything was organized and tidy. He wondered whether a maid had been hired to do the job? Nothing seemed apparent to the eye. In quiet reflection Detective James thought back to the time he spent in the bush with his father. They never left a trace. Refuse was either burnt or ported back to its source and thrown out with the garbage. Sergeant James glanced over at the open fireplace and walked over to the area. He bent forward and examined the metal grate which suspended the wood from the base. He traced his finger over the metal and could see a fine film of ashes covering his skin. He pulled the damper abruptly and loose soot fell from the chimney. Detective James moved back, he didn't want to inhale the substance. The suspects had been burning something, the soot had not yet crystallized. He once more rattled the metal damper. A partially charred piece of paper floated to the grated area. He bent over and studied the charred remains. To the visible eye, it was a section of a map faded by the heat. He could not interpret the names of the places. Carefully, he removed the paper and placed it in a small padded folder, then inserted it into a plastic bag. He would have it evaluated by the Forensic unit. Sergeant James would not share the evidence with his partner. From this point forward he would retain all information. There had been a leak in the operation, and he wasn't certain if he could trust Sergeant Cormick? Quietly, he moved from the basement to the main floor.

"Nothing down there Ralph! Let's get out of here." The detectives nodded to the on duty officer as they walked past his car. He was too busy eating a large donut and didn't notice them leave. Sergeant James drove the short distance back to the precinct. Having parked the car, the two cops hurried into the building. Detective James asked his partner to wait in the office, then he made his way to the basement level. He entered the Forensics office. Scanning the area, he could see the forensic scientist evaluating something under a microscope. Sergeant James walked behind the counter and cleared his throat as he approached the scientist.

"Hi Peter, I've got something I'd like you to examine. I'm working on a case and thought you could help me out on this one. I have a charred piece of paper. It looks like a map, but I can't figure out the location? I want you to keep this information confidential."

"No problem Sergeant James!" The forensic scientist retrieved the charred map and placed it under the lens of his magnifying glass. Looking through the lens, he increased the intensity of the light.

"Yep looks pretty clear to me now. This is a map of Alberta, northern Alberta to be exact. I can see the name Cold Lake." He reached into a file drawer at the side of his desk and extracted some maps of the western province. Opening it to Alberta, he looked at the charred remains and then back at the intact map. "Yep this it, same place on the map. The area you are looking at is Cold Lake, Alberta," he said smiling.

Detective James thanked the scientist and walked briskly up the staircase. He would not share the information with Ralph Cormick but only show it to his captain. Entering his office, he could see Sergeant Cormick sitting at the desk reading a newspaper. As he approached his partner, an excited out of breath rookie ran into the room demanding they contact Superintendent Elliot immediately. Sergeant Cormick retrieved his cell phone and dialled the number to the superintendent's office. Detective James looked on as his partner nodded his head during the conversation and then deactivated the phone.

"They've got one of the mercenaries trapped! Let's move. They have him at Union station! The place is sealed off. When the undercover unit moved in on him, he wounded two of the officers", stated Sergeant Cormick in an excited voice. Both detectives ran for the exit. Within minutes they were on their way to Union station. Sergeant James activated the vehicle lights and held the pedal to the floor. Every second seemed like an hour in their bid to cover the distance. Not a word was shared between the detectives. Union station was now in sight, they could see uniformed officers scurrying. Detective James slammed down the brake, and the vehicle screeched to a halt. The two detectives bounded up the stairs and ran toward the building. The cop recognized the man yelling out orders.

"Any idea where he is Harry?" asked Sergeant James.

"Yea! The suspect was spotted running along the tracks near the repair shop. My men have the area surrounded. It's impossible to get out," he replied. Detective James quickly introduced his partner, then both men entered the station. They could hear the sergeant in charge, directing his orders.

"Now hear this. I'm Sergeant Brooks of the Tenth Precinct. The suspect has been spotted. He is holding up in the repair shop. Everyone is to proceed with due caution. The suspect is armed and dangerous." Detective James approached the sergeant holding the megaphone.

"I'm Sergeant James and this is Sergeant Cormick. We have been working on this case for about a month. We need this guy alive! He is wanted in connection with some terrorist activity." The sergeant eyed both men suspiciously as he looked at their badges.

"If you fellows are crazy enough to go in, that is your business. The suspect has already wounded two officers. My men are not crazy about rushing in, but we will provide you with back-up. I will contact my men, you have a five minute head start," he stated.

"You take the rear of the building Ralph, I'm going in through the front." Sergeant Cormick moved along the side of the building and around to the back. Detective James crept toward the opened door and looked into the blackness which stared back at him. He dropped to his knees and crept forward on his stomach. He would make himself as small a target as possible if the suspect initiated firing. He glanced backward at the cop partially hidden behind the railway ties. Detective James crept into the building and was swallowed by the darkness. He listened carefully but could not detect any sounds from within. Sergeant James knew he would have to penetrate deeper if he was going to catch a glimpse of the suspect.

The red Firebird fishtailed as the commander made the final turn. Within minutes he would be there. His foot pressed heavily on the gas pedal. Arriving at the congested intersection, the commander parked the vehicle in an alleyway closest to the Union station. He cautiously moved from the vehicle. His khaki military jacket concealed the automatic weapon. He retracted into the shadows of the building, as cops ran past him toward the warehouse.

Sergeant Cormick moved forward, ducking behind piled crates as he made his way into the rear entrance of the warehouse. A noise caught his attention. At the far end of the building, he could see a dark figure hobbling in his direction. Sergeant

Cormick scanned the area, now realizing he was alone against the terrorist. As the suspect moved closer, he yelled the order.

"I've got you covered! Drop your weapon or you're a dead man." Nervous anxiety froze each second as adrenalin pulsed through his body. Sergeant Cormick waited patiently for the sound of metal to echo off the floor. The gun did not drop as expected. Instead, the assailant dropped to his knees and let out a burst from his automatic weapon. Shots ricocheted off the crates behind Sergeant Cormick, the cop dove for cover. A figure moved behind him, but Sergeant Cormick did not see the silhouette in time. He only felt the heavy weight of the boot, as it crashed into his skull. Sergeant Cormick sensed the luminous figure above him, just as he passed into a state of unconsciousness.

"Hans it's me! I have everything under control. I've just put the cop down. Hurry toward me quickly," said the commander. The assailant hesitated, but then moved ever so cautiously with his gun still pointed at the dark figure. Suddenly, he lowered the weapon and placed it at his side. He recognized the commander.

"I didn't think you would come for me. I've been hit, but I think I'm okay," said the mercenary.

"We're getting out of here Hans." The mercenary sensed the weight of his body shift to the commander's shoulder. Both men, edged their way toward the rear of the building. The commander looked out at the darkened structures. He would use the shadows to make his way back to the vehicle. They moved slowly through the yard stopping when crackling sounds of portable radios were heard in the distance. Hans could see the red vehicle tucked behind the building. Moving slowly forward, the commander opened the rear door. The wounded mercenary was positioned on the seat. In the distance, the commander could hear commotion coming from the building. The Firebird's engine howled as he backed into the street. Picking his way through the congested area, he could hear the low deep gasps from the rear seat.

"Hang on Hans! I'll have you out of here shortly. I'll notify the men to get a doctor. You'll be out of this mess soon." From his rear view mirror, he could see the flashing lights of the police cruisers fading in the distance. The commander wondered whether he could get the wounded man back to the farm house in time. His son had lost a lot of blood and was almost comatose. His foot pressed down on the gas pedal as the Firebird entered the Gardiner Expressway. Within 10 minutes, they'd be heading west on the 401 and in an hour, back at the farmhouse.

CHAPTER 23

Lieutenant Brown sat at his desk staring at the sheets in front of him. Emerald Lee had vanished. The psychopathic killer had slipped through their fingers. A pawn shop dealer reported a man of Emerald's description talking to a waitress in front of Jim's restaurant. From his search of the website, psychopaths were described as solitary individuals who didn't maintain relationships. He would do a follow up just in case the researchers had made an error. He would share the information with Dr. Allen and get his opinion. He punched in the telephone number printed on the business card. Lieutenant Brown asked for the psychologist's extension. The secretary in the Forensic Unit informed him Dr. Allen was away on holidays.

"What about Dr. Peterson?" asked Lieutenant Brown.

"Dr. Peterson is not here, but she left a number for you Lieutenant Brown." He hoped Dr. Peterson would be able to provide him with more information. As he punched in the numbers, once again he realized his oversized fingers made the execution of the task difficult. After waiting a few seconds, a voice at the other end answered.

"This is Lieutenant Brown! I was given your number by the secretary at the hospital, I hope you don't mind me calling you at home. I have some questions regarding the Lee case."

"What are your questions?" she asked.

"You already know Emerald Lee is still at large. I have been pouring over the data but something doesn't add up. A pawn shop dealer reported seeing a man who fit Lee's description talking to a waitress, then leaving with her. From the data I have been examining, psychopaths don't have intimate relationships. I was wondering if there are any exceptions? I have done an APIC search and discovered the waitress doesn't have a criminal record. Is there a probability she could be involved with a psychopath? I would like to bring her in for interrogation," said Lieutenant Brown.

"Why don't you come to my residence detective, I want to share some information with you." Lieutenant Brown accepted the invitation and wrote down the address. Dr. Peterson lived in an apartment not far from the Bingham Neurosurgical Centre. It would only take about 10 minutes to get to her residence.

As he drove from the parking lot, Lieutenant Brown didn't notice the black limousine following in the distance. He travelled along the expressway and then made a left at the exit in the direction Dr. Peterson had given. His car made one more turn and pulled into the parking lot of the high-rise condominium tower. From the back seat of the limousine, the occupants watched as Lieutenant Brown entered the foyer. The detective glanced at the name plate, then pressed a button. He waited for a brief period, then entered the building. Walking toward the opened door of the elevator, he entered and depressed the key pad. The door of the elevator closed. Lieutenant Brown listened to the soft tunes of the classical music as he ascended to the tenth floor. The door of the elevator opened, he glanced at the numbers on the wall and walked in the direction of her unit. He pressed the door bell and waited briefly. Dr. Peterson opened the door and greeted the detective.

"How have you been Lieutenant Brown?" she asked smiling.

"Depressed! We almost had Emerald Lee but lost him. I haven't had any leads in the last week, with the exception of the pawn shop dealer who reported a man resembling Lee talking to a waitress. I want to bring her in for interrogation but have to be certain she is involved. These things can backfire and I don't want it messing up my chance of promotion," responded Lieutenant Brown.

"Don't take this case personally detective. From our evaluation, we know that Emerald Lee is a clever fellow, possibly one of the brightest psychopaths we evaluated at Bingham. I have read Dr. Allen's report," she smiled.

"Dr. Allen briefed me on the results of the psychological evaluation," responded Lieutenant Brown.

"That is why I invited you here. I've got some information I want to share. It is highly confidential. If word gets out, it could create some controversial problems for the Bingham Neurosurgical Centre. You have been making a lot of statements to the press. You have been telling the media it is only a matter of time before Emerald Lee is caught. I think that is a mistake," she said.

"What do you mean?" snapped Lieutenant Brown.

"There is no need to get defensive. I'm not trying to initiate an argument. All I'm saying is Emerald Lee is not stupid. By making demeaning statements about this fellow will only draw attention to yourself. I'm just asking you to downplay this case for a while. The neurosurgeons at Bingham have taken care of the problem," she added.

"What are you saying Dr. Peterson?"

"I'm not sure if you have done your research on the Bingham facility. However, I'm going to give you some facts which I believe will assist in re-evaluating this case. As you know, our institution is funded by the Federal Bureau of Corrections and Rehabilitation. A board of directors, report to the chairman of this Bureau. About five years prior, a decision had to be made regarding criminal offenders. Of special interest to our board were psychopaths. From the research which had been collected, there didn't seem to be any way of treating these people. In the end the board made a decision to do something about psychopathic offenders. The death penalty had been vetoed. Permanent incarceration of each psychopath was costing the city $100,000 dollars in taxpayer's money per year.

We knew the money could be better used in medical research, so a decision was made to permanently treat these offenders," she stated factually.

"What are you talking about Dr. Peterson?" asked the detective.

"Lieutenant Brown you won't have any way of verifying the facts I'm about to give you, so you will have to trust me. A group of medical specialists were assembled to deal with the psychopaths. From the data we had evaluated on Positron Emission Tomography, we found psychopaths had a defective brain. Their disorder prevented them from engaging in socially acceptable behaviour. In other words, brain damage did not allow them to appreciate moral and social decision making. One of our specialists has studied psychopaths and written extensively on this subject. In the end, we had a crucial decision to make, one which involved re-programming psychopaths. I'm not sure what you know about nanotechnology but this field involves the interface of bioengineering and computer technology. Medical researchers have learned ways of circumventing damaged brain areas by reconnecting them or as you might have it re-wiring areas of the brain. The technique involves inserting programmed silicon chips into the defective brain and fusing the chips to neural fibres. In other words, by crosswiring the defective brains of psychopathic patients, we have been able to remove their homicidal impulses. This might seem a bit sci-fi to you Lieutenant Brown, but our research over the last five years has shown a 99% hit rate. The patients you saw marching around in a zombie-like-state at Bingham, had all been nanowired. They had been effectively treated and were going to be returned to jail. Once their sentences were up they would be released, no longer a threat to society. Emerald Lee had also been put under the knife, his brain had been nanowired. Although we were not able to complete all of our testing, the results were promising. My job at Bingham was to monitor the offenders. The tapes I collected on Emerald Lee indicate the operation was successful. After surgery, he was returned to the forensic unit. I ran him through a series of experiments. When he was exposed to violent films, he showed the expected response. Lee experienced a migraine headache, followed by nausea and vomiting. I don't know if you ever saw the film A Clockwork Orange? Our medical research has created the same effect without the implementation of drugs or aversive conditioning. In the end, we have achieved the same positive results. Isn't that what rehabilitation is all about Lieutenant Brown, getting the criminals off the streets?" she asked.

Detective Brown was mesmerized by her statement, but could not immediately respond. Dr. Peterson had discussed advanced medical research as an alternate way of dealing with psychopathic offenders. His mind raced forward to the future, criminal behaviour would be controlled through medical procedure, a smile crossed his face.

"This is much better than .45 calibre therapy Dr. Peterson. But how can you be sure the technique worked with Emerald Lee? After he escaped from the hospital there was an incident in which he attacked a police officer. If Emerald Lee had been cured, wouldn't he have refrained from the attack?" asked the curious cop.

"Good point Lieutenant Brown! I have reviewed the tapes of Emerald Lee's escape from Bingham. I can show you footage of an incident which took place during his escape. Prior to attacking the guards, I have footage which shows Emerald Lee clutching his head almost like he is having a seizure, then vomiting after the attack. His physical assault on the guards was minimal. Most dangerous psychopaths would have killed their opponent. If you examine the situation regarding the police officer, you know Emerald Lee had the officer's gun and could have killed him, but didn't. If you undertake a forensic re-evaluation of the crime, you will find other clues. If you re-visit the crime scene, it is my hunch you will retrieve Emerald Lee's vomit laced with his saliva and DNA. This will prove to you, he is currently responding to the re-programming procedure. Any violence he conjures up, or is about to engage in, creates violent migraine headaches, dizziness and sickness. These factors will condition him to refrain from aggressive activity. His brain will be kindled to respond in a positive way. Mr. Lee will no longer pose a risk to society. In time, he may even become a contributing societal member. I know you are a smart man, we have checked you out. We like your philosophy regarding criminal offenders. You have achieved success in this city and by next year will be captain of your precinct. In time, the Federal Bureau of Corrections and Rehabilitation will ensure you become the mayor of this great city. With people like yourself in a position of power, our goals will be furthered. We are interested in a community which is safe for its citizens. If it means nanotechnology for criminal offenders, so be it. I don't want you to give me any opinion on what I have said today. I want you to think of the implications. I want you to forget about further statements to the press. No more reporting on the Emerald Lee case. Just go about your job as usual. Someone will be in contact with you in the near future. And remember, your captain is stepping down shortly and you will be installed as the new captain of the police department," she stated factually.

Detective Brown was stupefied by her remarks. He nodded in acceptance and thanked her. He left the apartment, still flabbergasted by her statements. He would help them with their model of rehabilitation. Detective Brown would be ready to go the distance. He would embrace their plan and say nothing more to the press. He would wait and see if the future unfolded as she had predicted. If things went accordingly, Detective Brown would be ready to take on his new role. In time, he would be ready to assist the Federal Bureau of Corrections and Rehabilitation in rectifying the criminal element. Each surgical operation would be performed with precision and crime would be controlled. No longer would he have to resort to strong arm tactics.

As Lieutenant Brown left the apartment building, the occupants of the limousine sank into their seats to avoid detection. The cop got into his vehicle and drove in the direction of his apartment building located in Queens. Max Winters ordered the driver to follow. Twenty minutes later, they watched from the black limousine as the detective slammed the door of his vehicle and entered the building. Max Winters lowered the window slowly and looked out.

"If he gets in the way again Crosby, I want you to take him out. I have been given direct orders from the top. Detective Brown is a detriment to our operation. Do you understand?" he asked.

CHAPTER 24

Sergeant James met with his police chief and discussed the new evidence. They now had a lead from the charred map. He shared his hunch about the possibility someone in the police force had been passing information to the terrorists. It wouldn't be the first time a cop had infiltrated, and sold out to the other side. Sergeant Cormick had been hospitalized, but would recover from his concussion suffered at the hands of the terrorists. After a lengthy interaction with his boss, Detective James convinced the police chief to allow him to continue with the operation.

He had followed up on the evidence and discovered a Sabrecraft 40A had been chartered in Toronto and landed in a remote airfield not far from Humboldt, Saskatchewan. According to the information, three people were on board when the small jet landed. Detective James had contacted the airfield, and learned one of the men fit the description of Emerald Lee. An Air Canada flight was leaving for Saskatoon at 10:00 a.m., he would be on it.

Sergeant James made the turn on Airport road and proceeded to Terminal 1. He parked his car in the underground lot adjacent to the terminal. Walking briskly from the elevator, he entered the main lobby. The flight clerk smiled at him as he presented his ticket. She asked for his documents and after quickly inspecting his photo id, handed the cards back to him.

"You'll have to hurry sir, the plane leaves in 30 minutes."

Sergeant James did not waste any time but hurried to the waiting plane. He presented his ticket and boarded the aircraft. In approximately three hours, he would be in Saskatoon. Then, he would rent a vehicle which would take him to the Humboldt airfield. It wouldn't be the first case he had been assigned to undertake on his own. In time, he would check his hunches and attempt to piece the information together. Someone was feeding information to the suspects. The terrorists always seemed to be one step ahead. After he solved this case, Detective James would go looking for the infiltrator. He walked down the aisle and located his seat. No one had been assigned to the seat next to him. Sergeant James would use the extra space to spread out his file notes. The three hours on the aircraft would allow him to re-evaluate the information. The cop knew it was just a matter of time before he pieced together the data.

CHAPTER 25

Detective Brown's vehicle moved with ease along the freeway. There were certain advantages to the early morning travel in New York. As he drove the distance to his office, he reflected back to his first encounter with Emerald Lee. Initially, he wanted to solve the problem with .45 calibre therapy. The neurosurgeons at the Bingham Neurosurgical Centre had provided an alternate solution. Emerald Lee would no longer be the focus of his investigation. According to Dr. Peterson, the psychopath had been effectively shut down. It would just be a matter of time before Emerald Lee faltered and returned to custody.

Lieutenant Brown would now focus on Brenda Williams. She had been spotted talking to a man who resembled Lee, then leaving the restaurant with him. If he could crack her under interrogation, then she might provide him with Lee's location. The detective would use her as bait. He would comply with Dr. Peterson's request and not make any further statements to the press. In time, if Dr. Peterson's promises were kept, he would achieve a position of power. As captain of the precinct he would take charge, and assist the Bureau of Corrections and Rehabilitation in changing the criminal element.

Detective Brown parked his vehicle in front of Jim's restaurant. From his position, he could see the owner moving near the counter. A waitress pounded on the door and was let in by the beer-bellied man with a stained white apron. The sign on the door indicated the restaurant was now open. The morning crowd started filtering into the establishment. It was time to make his move. The door of the unmarked vehicle opened allowing Lieutenant Brown to slide from the cloth seat. The police officer glanced at his surroundings before he entered the building. He scanned the dining area, then walked over to a seat in Brenda Williams' section of the restaurant. Just as he seated himself in the booth, the waitress approached.

"I'll have a coffee, make it black," he stated.

The waitress sauntered to the counter and poured a coffee. From her profile, Detective Brown knew she was the one he was after. With a steaming coffee in her tray, the waitress returned to his table. The detective looked up at her and smiled as he flashed his badge.

"I'm Lieutenant Brown! I work for the New York police department and have a few questions to ask you. I can do it civilly right here or take you down to the precinct for interrogation. What is your name?" he asked smiling.

"Brenda Williams," she responded.

"I'd appreciate it if you would make it quick. My boss doesn't like me spending too much time with the customers," she said calmly. Detective Brown couldn't believe it. She had acted indifferently and requested he get on with his job. She had it together for someone suspected of aiding and abetting a known felon.

"We've been investigating a felon who escaped from the Bingham Neurosurgical Centre. A citizen reported seeing you talking to him, and then leaving Jim's restaurant with him," he said factually. Lieutenant Brown would soon know whether his hunch was correct. He studied her carefully for signs of nervous tension.

"Gee I don't know who that could be," she responded. The detective pulled a picture from his wallet.

"Maybe this snapshot will jar your memory," he added. Brenda looked at the picture then shook her head.

"He looks like a rock star. No, I don't think I know him," she smiled.

"Are you sure?" asked Lieutenant Brown.

"I've seen a lot of guys who could pass for this guy's double. There are all kinds of weirdos around here. Maybe the citizen who saw me, thought I was talking to your suspect, but maybe I was just giving him directions," she added.

"What about the guy you left with?" he asked.

"What if I went with him for a drink at Spacey's. He told me his name was Jim Michaels, I haven't seen him since. He never gave me his address," she responded.

"I could get a search warrant right now and go to your place. Forensics would dust the place for fingerprints. We could hold you in custody until we get the evidence. I'm giving you a chance. I don't know if you are mixed up with Emerald Lee? If you only had a one time fling with him that's your business. However, if you are withholding information I will charge you with aiding and abetting a known felon. You could do some serious time in jail. Level with me right here and right now, or you are going down," said the agitated cop. Lieutenant Brown watched her body composure. He had hit a visible nerve. From the tension she was now exhibiting, he knew the waitress would soon cave in.

"Okay! I did have a drink with the guy and he did go home with me, so what if I screwed him. Is there any law against that? How did I know he was a wanted felon. I only spent an evening with him and haven't seen him since. I'd be happy to go down to the precinct and make a statement. When do you want me to come? I live at 59 Batten Drive, Apartment 15, you can check me out. If you will let me get back to my job, I will be happy to come to your office at 3:00 p.m. when I get off work. You can keep an eye on me," she stated nervously.

"I'm happy you are willing to cooperate Ms. Williams. I want you in my office promptly at 3:30 p.m. If you don't show up, I will have you arrested," stated the detective. He paid for his coffee. As he got up to leave, he noticed Brenda Williams was visibly upset by the confrontation. Agitated, she almost dropped the coffee cup as she retrieved it from the table.

Lieutenant Brown drove back to the precinct in silence. He would get a search warrant. When she arrived at his office, he would first interrogate her and then Brenda Williams would accompany him and the forensic team to her apartment. They would dust her apartment for evidence. He entered the precinct building and proceeded to his office. As he sat at his desk, he activated the computer and punched in her name, little information appeared on the screen. She did not have a criminal record and had never even received a parking ticket. He wondered whether there would be corroborating evidence linking her to Emerald Lee?

He left his office and headed for the coffee machine. The computer search would require a few more minutes, and then he would have the complete profile. Two uniformed cops passed him in the hallway. He nodded and inquired about their families. It wasn't that he cared, but simply because it was good policy as their superior officer. If Dr. Peterson's information was accurate, he would soon be running the precinct. With his coffee in hand, he walked back to his office. The printer was rattling out the information when he arrived. Lieutenant Brown grabbed the sheets and studied them. Brenda Williams had moved to New York city from Toronto. Lieutenant Brown wondered how she had obtained her Green card to work in the States. As he read further, he noticed she had been married to an American soldier who had died in the Gulf War. A sense of nostalgia quickly overtook him. He cleared his throat as he reflected on his fallen comrades. Lieutenant Brown's unit had seen combat on the front line and some of his friends had been killed in the same war. He experienced some compassion for Brenda Williams but quickly replaced the thought with his task at hand. He would have the Forensics team inspect her place. If he found she was lying, he would shake her down.

Dr. Peterson had asked him to stay clear of the case, but she hadn't said anything about Brenda Williams. There were many lose ends, he needed a vantage point. He needed something to solve the case. Brenda Williams would provide the details so he could complete this one. Then, he would be ready to move forward with his career. First, he would become precinct captain, and in time, mayor of the city. Lieutenant Brown experienced a brief sense of guilt having agreed to cooperate with the psychologist. She was a member of a clandestine operation. The medical specialists at the neurosurgical centre had performed questionable surgical operations. The prisoners had been operated on without consent. He reflected on the scenario but came to the conclusion their operatives were similar to his objectives. Lieutenant Brown needed to be in control, he wanted the vantage point. If they came through, he would attain a status of power few could ever hope to achieve. The way he saw it, he was either with them or some other member of the police force would be given the option. He wanted to be on their team. Dr. Peterson mentioned the board of directors had done a detailed analysis of his background. His record was clean and he had many commendations for upholding the law. He knew they had made a good choice when they selected him. He would not let the Bureau down.

The detective spent his day working on the case. He would return to the Pawn shop after he secured a statement from Brenda Williams. He'd have to be sure before putting pressure on her. If Brenda had lied to him, she would regret it. He had used dirty tactics more than once to solve a case. Once again he would use pressure to obtain the truth. The wary cop looked down at the cold black coffee in his cup. Slowly, he brought the thick putrid substance to his lips, he winced but managed to swallow the liquid. He raised himself from the chair and walked toward the computer room. As he looked in, he noticed the technician thumbing through a printout.

"Hey Bruce, you got anything on my case?" he asked. The technician startled, as he looked up at the detective.

"I sure have Lieutenant Brown! Look at this."

Detective Brown's surprised expression was quickly replaced with a serious frown as he browsed through the information directed from Interpol. A high priority alert had been sent out. The detective's eyes widened as he mouthed the names of the terrorists. I knew there was something about Lee I didn't like. So that's his game. He's not only a psychopath but involved with a terrorist group. Lieutenant Brown read the names of the other suspects. The terrorists were in the country to do a job but the details weren't clear. Lieutenant Brown hurried back to his office. He walked to the cabinet, retrieving Lee's file, then dialled the number.

"This is Lieutenant Brown speaking, put me through to the captain," he said. The secretary's voice was immediately replaced with that of the superior officer. The detective provided the details of the case stating he would soon be interrogating Brenda Williams. The captain listened carefully to the facts and then ordered Lieutenant Brown to arrest Brenda Williams immediately. She was to be brought in for questioning. The detective hung up the phone and radioed the dispatcher to send two officers to Jim's restaurant to arrest Brenda Williams. Lieutenant Brown sat at his desk and studied the file. The officers would soon bring her to his office, he would start the interrogation. He would not go easy on her, but would use all the dirty tactics he had learned. He would get the search warrant and then send Forensics to her apartment to look for evidence.

CHAPTER 26

Sergeant James arrived at the Saskatoon airport and rented an SUV. He quickly covered the short distance from Saskatoon to the remote airfield in Humboldt, Saskatchewan. According to the airfield controller, the small Sabrecraft jet had landed the day before and refuelled. The suspects had flown in a northwesterly direction. Two RCMP officers had arrived by Cessna aircraft earlier that day and left in pursuit of the suspects. Detective James walked into the terminal building and obtained the suspect's flight plan. According to the filed information, their destination was Edmonton. The airfield controller had found the information a little odd because they had not flown west.

"What about the RCMP officers? Which direction did they fly?" asked the detective.

"They were flying to Calgary."

"But didn't they ask you the direction the suspects had taken?" asked Sergeant James.

"Nope! They didn't ask, so I didn't tell them," said the man. If the information given by the airfield controller was correct, the RCMP officers would be flying in the wrong direction. Detective James wondered why the suspects had flown in a northwesterly direction. If his hunch was correct, they would be heading for the airfield in Cold Lake, Alberta. Their target would be the military base. He needed to get there fast but it would take him too long to drive. He walked into the small terminal building and approached a lady seated behind the desk.

"I'd like to go to Cold Lake. Is there a company here flying charters?" he asked. The horned rimmed lady looked up at him.

"Nope! But I can take you if the price is right! I have a small Cessna, but it can easily make the trip."

"I will pay the going rate plus an extra $100 if we can leave shortly," said the detective.

"Consider it done. Be ready to leave in ten minutes," said the lady.

Detective James walked out to his vehicle and removed his duffle bag from the trunk. Inside was the necessary arsenal if he had to resort to violence. He walked over to the plane and examined its structure. The fuselage seemed in good condition, even though the plane was an older model. Within minutes the pilot arrived. She was dressed in flying gear with radio transmitter connected to her leather flying hat. Climbing up to the pilot's seat, she turned the ignition. At first, the prop sputtered but then the engine fired, cranking the propeller at an accelerated rate.

"I've got an oversized blade on this baby, so don't worry if she howls. She's almost ready to go. I keep her in good shape. You never can tell when an emergency comes up. I'll give her five minutes to warm up and we'll be off," remarked the pilot. Detective James fastened his seat belt.

"You can put that on if you want, but you won't be needing it. I may not look much like a pilot, but I'm one of the best. I can fly a hell of a lot better than most fellahs around here. Relax sonny, this is going to be one of the best flights you ever had. Now quit clenching your fists, it makes you look like you've got a case of the jitters," said the pilot.

"When you return to the airport would you do me a favour and contact Expedition Rentals and ask them to pick up my SUV. It's parked in front of the terminal building. I'm not sure when I'll make it back this way," stated Sergeant James. He produced the key ring and handed it to the pilot.

"It'll probably cost you a heck of a lot of money to have them pick it up. For another hundred bucks, I'll have my son drive it to the Saskatoon airport," said the pilot. Detective James smiled at her. He dug into his pocket and withdrew the bills and handed them to her.

"I can see you are a real entrepreneur," he said.

"Now don't go using any of them high fluting words with me son. I'm a down to earth business woman. I just know a good situation when I see one. If I have a chance to make a few bucks then I take on a job. With the cost of living these days, it's hard to make ends meet. Those taxation people are always trying to get every red cent I earn. At least by doing these extra jobs, I have some write offs," she added.

"Good idea," replied the detective.

"You told me you were a cop. Are you after criminals?" she asked.

"Yes, but I can't go into detail. Do me a favour and don't mention this flight to anyone. It is important I keep this classified. It could prevent some people from getting hurt," he added.

"Don't worry about me. My lips are sealed. If I can be of service, I'll do everything I can to assist you on this mission," she said with a wink.

"I'm tired and would like to take a short nap. Wake me when we get to the Cold Lake airfield. You might need clearance to land. Give them the information listed on this piece of paper. It should make things a little easier," he said. The pilot studied the words and mouthed a code name. It didn't make any sense but it wasn't her concern. As the plane left the runway, she looked at her gauges. It would be approximately a two hour flight. She would arrive well ahead of sundown. The pilot looked over at the detective, he was slouched back in his seat. The officer closed his eyes as the aircraft banked and headed in a northwesterly direction. In his semi-conscious state, his mind wandered back to earlier events. Only six weeks had passed since his involvement on this case. He'd worked on many undercover operations but none had gone down this way. Detective James had a difficult time relying on others, he had always worked alone. His thoughts drifted back to the events which had almost lead to the demise of his partner. He attempted to repress the memory into his unconscious mind. Once again, it was working its way to the present. The voice called out his name. Gun shots echoed and he could still hear the plea for help. Luckily, the suspects hadn't killed Sergeant Cormick. The image was replaced with another as he felt himself drifting into a light sleep. She called out loudly in his direction. He caught a glimpse of her hand flailing at the surface of the turbulent water. Their canoe bobbed on the surface, he reached desperately for her. Frantically, he dove into the depths of the cold black water but returned exasperated. A few seconds before she had been there, and now she was gone. An arm reached out and grabbed the breathless swimmer. The rescuer fought with the half-crazed victim and finally secured him to the lifeboat. Sergeant James bolted upright in his seat, as he looked nervously around the cockpit.

"No need to worry son. We just hit some air turbulence. It happens this time of the year. Sometimes you can drop a few hundred feet. I had to descend quickly to break the grip of the air pocket. In about a half-hour we'll be landing. I already called the airfield and gave them the code. They have cleared us for landing," she said.

Detective James looked out from his window at the ground below. Much of the land mass was covered by black spruce trees in this northerly latitude. He could see some vehicles moving below on the small tertiary roads. In the west, the last rays of the setting sun shone above the horizon.

"Will you be staying in Cold Lake over night?" he asked.

"I'm not that kind of girl," said the aging horned rimmed pilot as she let out a boisterous laugh.

"Just kidding, actually sonny, I've got no problem flying this aircraft in the dark. As soon as I let you off, I'm heading back home. Should be there by nine if the weather holds up. Betsy is one of the best Cessna's I've ever owned. I don't have to gas her up. I have more than half a tank and that should easily get me back to Humboldt. It looks like we are going to hit some air turbulence, fasten your seatbelt quickly," she said. Detective James reached for the buckle and snapped it shut. Almost immediately, the small aircraft shook violently and dropped. He could feel his stomach jolt upward then settle back into his body cavity.

"What the hell was that?" he asked nervously.

"Clear air turbulence. Its one of the most dangerous things a pilot can run into this time of year. Larger aircraft can get shaken apart by that stuff. We were lucky and only hit the tail end. We're almost ready to land. I've been given clearance, here goes nothing," she said. Just ahead, he could see dim lights lining the airfield. The plane circled once and then made its descent. She fought hard with the controls to steady the wings. The aircraft bounced once and then settled down onto the tarmac surface. It sped to the far end of the runway before slowing. The pilot then steered the plane in the direction of the hangar.

"How's that for landing?" she asked calmly.

"Couldn't be better. Thanks again for flying me here," he replied. Sergeant James removed his bag from the back seat and jumped onto the asphalt below. His legs felt like rubber on the solid pavement. Quickly, he regained his equilibrium.

"I hope you get them," said the pilot.

"Thanks," he replied. Detective James walked over to the airfield attendant who was quickly approaching. He flashed his badge.

"My name is Sergeant James. A jet landed at this airport yesterday," he stated authoritatively. Detective James described one of the suspects in detail and presented a picture of Emerald Lee.

"Now let me see. Yea a Sabrecat did land here yesterday with three men on board. This picture looks like the younger fellah. There was also an older man with greying hair and one guy who could have been about 40. They were dressed in army fatigues. Almost looked like they were military men. I overheard one of the guys talking about a contract at the Cold Lake military base. I thought it odd they landed here if they were doing some work for the military. Shouldn't they have landed on the military base? They unloaded some wooden crates. A guy in a white van was here to pick them up. The older man told me they were driving into town," he added.

"Have you got any vehicles for rent?" asked the detective.

"No I don't, but I could sell you an old vehicle I have been restoring. It's over in my shop. I was going to paint it, but you can have her for $500.00 dollars."

"Consider it sold!" said Sergeant James. He extracted his wallet and placed five crisp $100 bills in the extended hand. Detective James walked over to the terminal warehouse and looked at the 1980 Mustang. It had seen better days, but would provide him with the transportation needed as he sought out the suspects. He slid across the soiled cloth and inserted the key into the ignition. The motor started quickly. He noticed a map on the console and studied it. He traced his finger over the map. Half-way down the page, he recognized the name the groundsman had mentioned.

"Primrose Weapons Range," he muttered to himself. Hadn't he read something about it in the Toronto newspaper. He traced his finger over the map, just southeast of Calgary, he saw another familiar name. Detective James quickly ruled out the southeasterly base as the suspects probable destination. If they had wanted access to the range, they would have flown to Calgary. The suspects probably filed the Calgary destination with the airport in Humboldt to throw the police off course. The RCMP officers were probably now in Calgary. Detective James wondered if they would correct their error. A plan was put in motion. As he left the airport, Detective James knew time was of the essence. He would have to get to the military base so he could inform the commanding officer.

CHAPTER 27

He cupped his hands to his mouth and called out her name. His voice did not penetrate the loud rumble of the crowd. As he fought his way through the pedestrians, Emerald Lee could see her disappearing in the distance. Frantically, he thrashed his way forward and edged closer toward her. Emerald could almost see her now. His name was being called from the distance. It was getting louder, he jolted from the semi-conscious state. He sat upright on his cot. He was having the same repeated nightmare. In the distance, he could hear the commander's voice growing louder.

"Emerald get the hell down here!" yelled the commander. He sprung from his cot and stepped onto the carpet beside his bed. Instinctively, he laced up his boots. Before the commander could bellow once more, Emerald was down the stairs and walking toward the table. He seated himself and retrieved the cup of steaming coffee placed in front of him.

"Let me go over the plans once more. According to what the major said, the young pilot attends church Sunday at ten o'clock. He returns about eleven thirty, does a few things around the house and then goes to the military base to use the exercise room. He returns to his place about four, has supper and stays home for the evening. The plan is simple. I'm going to pose as a telephone repairman. I'll cut the line outside his place, and mention we have been having problems. I'll wire his land phone, when he uses it, he'll get electrocuted," said the commander.

Emerald Lee reflected back over the events which had taken place during his mercenary service with the European Liberation Order. He had done questionable things. His job had taken him into some of the most covert of operations. Land mines, car bombs, gasoline laced light bulbs had all been used as his modus operandus. He had caused untold destruction and suffering. Some, he believed deserved the fate, they had carved out their destiny for themselves. But others were victims, merely bystanders in his wrath of destruction. Reflecting over the events which had shaped his life, he was filled with anxiety and sadness. The migraine headache had once again pierced his temple. The excruciating pain surfaced from a deep recess in the region above his right ear. He rubbed at his head and rotated his neck to ease the pain. Images of his targets flashed to the present like omnipresent visual hallucinations. The visions were etched deep in his mind. He could hear the victims screaming as their torched bodies burned. He could smell human flesh ravaged by flames. A feeling of disgust and revulsion arose inside of him. In the pit of his stomach an unsavoury liquid was boiling, he fought to keep the fluid inside. As he glanced upward, Emerald could see the commander's lips move but his voice was garbled. Panic emerged in his brain, Emerald Lee could only stare with confused thoughts.

He reflected on the job at hand. What if the missiles were launched? The damage and destruction would be incalculable. Helpless victims would be killed by his brazen actions. Deep in thought, Emerald Lee knew he would have to stop the plan from unfolding. His electronic expertise would allow him a window in which he could prevent the human misery. He thought back to his relationship with Brenda. Somewhere in the depth of his mind, evil fought to gain control. He could only stare blankly ahead as the electrical energy transfixed him into a hypnotic trance. Emerald Lee could hear his name being called as he stared blankly ahead but could not pull himself back from the abyss of despair which separated his emotions from thoughts.

"Emerald, are you with us?" blurted the commander loudly. For a brief moment Emerald Lee had entered a different realm one which bordered on confusion. He experienced a sense of nausea. His thoughts had been separated into a multitude of fractious events. Anxiety and guilt emerged from an unknown entity. Emerald Lee felt sick to his stomach. He glanced up at his commander and experienced a sense of revulsion.

"And where do I come into the picture?" asked Emerald still traumatized by his flashbacks.

"Major Hathaway will request a change in plans when the young pilot does not show up. Steve will be called in as the replacement. You will be riding in the trunk of his vehicle. When the other pilot enters the hangar, you will take him out and put his body in the trunk of the vehicle. Once you have loaded the missile heads on the jet, you will act as the co-pilot. Steve will get clearance from Major Hathaway. Remember no slip ups. Are there any questions? Okay let's load the equipment. Make sure everything is functional. Emerald, I want you to ensure the jamming device is hooked up properly. If the job isn't done right, the US military may be able to monitor the missiles from their Wyoming base. If that happens, it's over for us. Do you think you can handle it?" he asked.

"No problem!" replied Emerald.

"Steve any last questions?" asked the commander.

"No!" was the reply

"Once in flight, we will make our demands. The US military will be notified of the probable attack if they do not meet our request. We will give them two hours to wire the money to an Offshore account. In the event the transaction is not made, they will be faced with the consequences. I don't think we will have to release the missiles. The US military is aware of the destructive capabilities of these weapons. They will realize it is in their best interest to meet our demands," he said.

Emerald Lee had made a proactive decision. He knew there would be no missiles released, and there would be no destruction. He had the expertise to sabotage the operation by altering the electronics. In the event the missiles were launched, he would set the guidance system so the missiles would crash after being fired. He would also dismantle the warheads. When the missiles made contact, there wouldn't be any explosion. He would have to get out immediately after the sabotage and return to New York. Contact had been lost with Brenda. When he got the chance, Emerald would make the call. They would rendezvous in New York, then leave the country together.

CHAPTER 28

Detective James looked out from his motel room. Little activity could be seen on the streets. According to the waitress at the restaurant, the only excitement in this isolated northern Alberta town happened on a Saturday night. Military men from the nearby Primrose Airbase would come to town and get drunk. They'd get into fights with the locals and someone would get busted up. The RCMP officers would drag the drunken brawling men off to jail.

He looked closely at the map. The military base was located ten miles from town. Detective James wondered if the suspects would make their attempt on the airbase. He would visit the site and attempt to convince the commanding officer to tighten security. Without hesitation, he dressed and left his motel room. He walked past the motel office and entered the door to his left. Few people occupied the large dining room. Detective James studied the room and decided on the table facing the main highway. Sitting at the table closest to the window, he looked out at the rising mist created by the slow moving trucks.

"Good morning sir, coffee?" asked the waitress.

"Yes please! Could I have the breakfast special, eggs lightly over," he replied waiting patiently as she filled his cup. The waitress jotted down the order. He sipped at the dark bitter liquid, sweetened with the brown crystals of demerara sugar found in the dispenser on the table. He thought it strange the proprietor of the restaurant would offer a choice of sweeteners. But this was the modern age and the owner was doing her best to cater to the needs of the clientele. Within five minutes the waitress returned with his order.

"Here you are sir, enjoy your meal."

"You probably live around here?" asked the detective.

"Yes I do. I was born and raised here. I tried living in Edmonton for a while but found it too fast and impersonal. I returned two years ago and enjoy the slow pace," she said with a smile.

"Have you noticed any strangers in town during the past few days?" he asked.

"No sir, I haven't! We generally get the locals in here for coffee. You're new in town, aren't you?" she asked.

"Yes I am. Just arrived last night. I'm looking for three friends. I was supposed to meet them at this motel. We're here to do some fishing. I tried calling them on my cell phone but I guess there isn't any service here."

"There have been quite a few people in town during the last month. Most of them with the press. They've been interviewing people. There seems to be quite some concern over the cruise missile test taking place at the Primrose Weapons range. People are pretty upset about the whole thing. The local natives have filed a grievance. They believe their people will be harmed by these weapons," she added.

"Cruise missile test?" asked Sergeant James coyly.

"Yes, you must have heard about it? It's been in the newspaper for months. Many people from northern Alberta have already opposed the test, it's supposed to happen on Monday. People are pretty scared about the whole thing. It probably has something to do with the satellite that crashed here last year. I guess they're worried a missile might come down on their houses. Can you believe it? The government is not even sure how safe the missiles are, and they are doing the testing in our backyard. They must think people in the north are stupid? Are you a reporter?" she asked.

"No just a cop on vacation. I'm trying to find my friends so we can do some fishing," he replied.

"There are lots of good lakes around here. My uncle Jimmy owns the Goosenda Lodge just outside of town. You should go and see him. He could set you up," she said.

"Thanks for the information. If you hear about three guys in a white van let me know. Just leave a message with the clerk at the front desk. I'm in room 102," he said.

"I'll probably be seeing you around" she smiled, then walked to the kitchen to retrieve another order.

Cruise missile test he thought to himself? Could that be it? Could the terrorists be attempting to sabotage the flight? Hadn't a terrorist group claimed responsibility for the explosion in Toronto? The Liddon plant had manufactured the guidance control system for the cruise missiles. He wondered if there was a link between his suspects and the terrorists who had made the attack on the plant. Detective James quickly wolfed down his food and gulped his coffee. He'd have to do some fast checking. The missile was scheduled to be tested in less than twenty-four hours.

Little traffic passed him, as he drove along Highway 55. In the distance, he could see the military base. He approached the sentry post and stopped the vehicle.

"Can I help you?" asked the armed officer.

"I'm Detective James! I would like to talk with your commanding officer," he said. The sentry glanced at the detective's badge and suspiciously inspected the vehicle he was driving.

"Is this your car? Sure looks in bad shape for a cop's car," he stated.

"I just flew into town, it was the only one I could get," he replied.

"I heard there were government cut-backs going on, but I didn't know they were this bad," said the guard as he smiled.

"Thanks, I appreciate your sense of humour," replied Sergeant James.

"Now what is your business?" asked the sentry.

"Classified!" replied the detective.

"I will inform Major Hathaway. He came in this morning, but I'm not sure where he is?" said the guard.

Through the plated window, Detective James could see the guard talking on his phone. He glanced in Detective James' direction then hung up the telephone. The military guard marched out from the building.

"He's in his office. Follow this road for about a kilometre. You'll see a brown building, give this pass to the guard in front of the major's headquarters. He'll show you to the office," said the sentry. Detective James took the slip and put it into his jacket pocket. He thanked the guard as the barricade lifted. As he drove the distance to the commander's office, he glanced at the hangars to his left. He wondered if the cruise missile aircraft was housed in the large buildings. Detective James drove another 200 metres, then parked his vehicle in front of the brown brick building. As he got out of his vehicle, he handed the guard the slip of paper.

"He's expecting you, come this way please," said the guard. The sentry led Detective James into the building.

"First door to the right sir," he shouted.

Detective James smiled at the attractive bespectacled secretary as he passed her desk. He knocked on the major's door and it immediately opened. An aging grey haired officer in his early sixties stood in the doorway.

"Come in Sergeant James! What can I do for you. I'm Major Hathaway", he said. The major walked over to a leather chair and sat down.

"Have a seat Sergeant James. What brings you to the base?" he asked inquisitively.

"I'm here on some classified business Sir. I have reason to believe some terrorists I have been following may attempt to sabotage this airbase. I uncovered some evidence indicating possible espionage. One of the suspects is wanted in connection with two homicides. We are particularly interested in this fellow because he killed a scientist connected with the manufacture of missile guidance devices at the Liddon plant in Toronto. The other two suspects have known links to the European Liberation Order, a mercenary faction involved in a number of sordid activities," he said factually. The major's mouth opened and his jaw dropped. His face made a transition from its ruddy complexion to ashen white.

"I can see you're visibly upset major. If my hunch is correct, there may be an attempt on this airbase in the next 24 hours," said the detective. The major's right hand reflexively went toward his mid-chest area as he massaged the large muscle over his heart. He walked briskly toward the cabinet located near the rear wall and withdrew a bottle of scotch. He poured the substance into a glass and brought it to his lips, quickly gulping down the tanned liquid.

"Would you like one Sergeant James?"

"No sir! I never drink on the job," he replied.

"I can see you have been busy detective. Are you working alone on this case?" asked the major coyly.

"I was working with a partner from the RCMP but he was injured in an altercation with the suspects. Currently, I'm working alone, but my captain knows I'm here," he replied. The major breathed a sigh of relief and returned to his leather chair.

"You did the right thing Sergeant James. I will inform the sentry to be on special alert. I'll also post guards at the periphery of the airbase. We can't be too careful in these times. If they have some interest in the cruise missile testing, we will be ready for them. How many did you say you were tracking?" he asked.

"Three major. I'm not certain whether they have linked up with others," replied the detective.

"I expect you will keep this information classified officer. I don't want anything getting out to the press until the cruise missile testing is completed. There is no telling what kind of panic this could cause," said the major.

"Yes, you can depend on me major."

"Now if you will excuse me for a minute, I'll make the necessary arrangements. Where are you staying in case I have to get in touch with you?" asked the major.

"The Bomark motel," replied Sergeant James.

"Make yourself comfortable detective, I have some calls to make." The major left the room and walked to another office. Entering the room, he locked the door behind him. Retrieving the telephone from the desk, he dialled a number stored in his memory centre.

"This is Major Hathaway calling. I'd like to talk to the commander!" he said abruptly. Major Hathaway waited impatiently, small beads of sweat collected on his brow. Finally a voice answered, the major's impulses could no longer be controlled.

"How the hell did you guys slip up? There is a cop in my office asking about the cruise missile test! He says he followed you out here. How could you have messed this one up?" said the major frantically.

"Impossible!" shouted the commander. Major Hathaway's ear resonated from the loud outburst.

"He seems to know everything about the operation! Has there been a leak at your end?" shouted Major Hathaway.

"We've got to get rid of him. We don't need him interfering with this operation. I'm making final preparation to eliminate the pilot. Get the cop off the base, find out where he is staying. We'll take care of him, then we'll head for the airbase," replied the commander. Major Hathaway slammed down the telephone. He wiped the sweat off his brow and returned to his office. As he entered the room, he could see Sergeant James staring at the bookcase.

"Come with me Sergeant." As they left the command post, Detective James noticed the military men marching in the direction of the hangar.

"As you can see Sergeant James I have doubled up the men on guard duty. As you drive from the airbase you will also notice there are more guards at the perimeter. The sentry post may ask for this when you leave. Hand it to him, there shouldn't be any problem getting off the base. I appreciate the time you have taken to investigate this matter. Sabotage is a serious crime. I will ensure no clandestine activity takes place on this airbase," he said. The major shook hands with the detective and followed him to the vehicle. As Sergeant James opened the door, he thanked the major for his cooperation. The major watched pensively as the police officer drove slowly toward the exit.

Major Hathaway re-entered the building and sat at his desk. Pouring a glass of scotch, he raised it to his lips and gulped it quickly. The major contemplated his predicament. He questioned his reasons for becoming involved in the operation. Somewhere in the depth of his mind, he contemplated his payout. He was scheduled to retire in six months but was unhappy with his pension. After 35 years of service, the military would only reward him with a meagre salary. It would not support the life style to which he had become accustomed. Greed and envy had taken control of him. He was angry at the system. They had not promoted him to the highest rank. For all his years of service, the military had rewarded him by re-locating him to a northern outpost. At first, he had accepted his fate, but with time had become resentful. Somewhere in the depth of his mind, rational thought had been replaced with malice. This was the ultimate reason for his betrayal. There could be no turning back. He would cooperate with the commander and fulfil his obligation. Major Hathaway would receive his final payment, and the $500,000 dollars would ultimately lead to a better retirement lifestyle. The mercenaries would disappear and he would travel to a warmer climate. Once again he dialled the familiar number. The phone rang three times and then a voice answered.

"This is Major Hathaway. The detective just left the airbase. He was returning to the Bomark motel. I don't think he's put the whole operation together. He seems pretty clever, so watch yourself. I don't want this one fouled up and make sure you bring my final $100,000 dollar payment. Go ahead with the plan as scheduled. I've given your man clearance to enter the base. The sentry post will be advised Steve has been assigned to evaluate the missile guidance system. Make sure you take out the pilot and Sergeant James."

CHAPTER 29

Detective James had driven back to the Bomark motel. He was seated in the dining room mulling over the facts of the case. A waitress approached his table.

"What would you like sir?" she asked.

"Give me a coffee with the special."

"Are you Sergeant James?"

"Yes," he replied curtly.

"Mandy told me to give this message to you." The waitress handed Detective James an envelope. He opened the letter and read the message.

"Sergeant James I did some checking after we spoke this morning. A guy who works for Northern Alberta Oil was out at the old Smith ranch located on Highway 101, north of town. He saw three guys at the abandoned Hogard ranch. They had a white van parked in front of the farmhouse. I hope the information is useful", Mandy.

Detective James shoved the letter in his coat pocket. He would finish his lunch and then drive out to the Hogard ranch. He wondered whether her information would be useful? Glancing at his watch, he realized it was almost three-thirty. He would have to hurry if he wanted to get there before sunset. Detective James wolfed down the T-bone steak, then rubbed the napkin over his mouth. He placed a twenty dollar bill on the table and hurried out to his car.

The sun was edging closer toward the horizon. A silhouette was cast by the rugged mountain range off in the distance. A shiver ascended his spine as he left the building. Detective James got into the mustang and followed the directions she had given him. The old abandoned ranch was just beyond the 106 intersection. Just over the rise in the hill, he could see two farms on opposite sides of the road. One was teaming with activity while the other one seemed deserted. He studied the name on the mail box, it was the one she had given him. He drove into the driveway and parked the vehicle in front of the barn. He would give the occupants of the dwelling a story about his car having problems, then would ask for their assistance. Looking up at the building, he could see a light. Detective James scanned the yard for signs of activity. Cautiously, he stepped from the cover of the pine trees in the front yard. He walked up to the front of the building and banged on the heavy wooden door. At first, he thought he could hear noises inside. As he strained his ears, he realized it was only the wind whistling through the needles of the pine trees in the front yard. Detective James looked out across the yard and studied the metal clad shed. He walked over and edged the door open. The building was empty with the exception of some wooden crates. On the side of the boxes were printed the words Electronics. He inspected the crates.

It was almost five o'clock. He would return to the Bomark motel and continue his investigation. According to the major, the military base was now on alert. Detective James wondered whether he should contact the RCMP. At this point, there wasn't enough evidence to arrest the suspects. Detective James decided to keep the operation quiet for now. Approaching the Bomark motel, he could see the neon lights illuminating the parking lot. Walking from his car, he approached his motel room and inserted the key into the lock. As he edged through the door, Sergeant James knew someone had been in his room. His dresser drawers were open and clothes scattered nearby. Without hesitation, he withdrew his handgun from his holster. He expected to see the enemy jump out at him. His temples pounded as blood pulsed through his cerebral arteries. With his left arm extended, he slowly pushed the door of the bathroom open, and scanned the room. He holstered his weapon, and returned to the entrance. Attaching the safety chain to the door, he walked toward the sofa and sank onto the cushions. Someone had been in his room searching for something, only Major Hathaway and his captain knew of his investigation.

CHAPTER 30

Major Hathaway could hear the phone ringing. He jumped up from his recliner and dropped the South American travel guide onto the coffee table.

"Who is it?" he blurted.

"It's the commander, I've run into some trouble."

"Did you eliminate them?" asked the major.

"The pilot wasn't a problem, he has been dispatched. We will be travelling to the base in the morning. I sent Steve and Emerald to the Bomark motel but they couldn't locate the cop. No one has seen him. He hasn't checked out yet. Later tonight, I will return to the motel and do the job. If the cop gets wind of this operation, he will notify the authorities. Don't worry major, I'll take care of everything."

The commander hung up the phone. He would wait for an hour, then return to the motel. Emerald and Steve were still loading the electronic equipment but would soon return. The commander reclined on the sofa and depressed the remote control button on the teleconverter. He watched the football players as they ran down the field. He reflected on his assignment. His mercenary group were like a team of players. They each had to carry out their job, if they were going to reach their goal. He chewed on the beef sandwich as he sipped his beer. He thought over the plan. It would work, as long as everyone did their part.

Emerald Lee had slipped up on his last assignment, it had almost jeopardized the operation. Lee had been acting oddly since his escape from the Bingham hospital. The commander couldn't pinpoint exactly what it was, but he knew Lee seemed different. If he failed at his job this time, the commander would personally eliminate him. But first, he would have to take care of Detective James. He made the telephone call to the Bomark motel. The desk clerk answered, stating she would put through the call. After a few minutes of waiting the clerk responded.

"I'm sorry sir, but he doesn't seem to be in his room."

"Could he be in the dinning room?" asked the commander.

"I don't think so sir. It's closed for the evening. Would you like to try later?" she asked.

"Yea sure, I'll do that." The commander slammed down the phone. There was nothing he could do at the moment. He would go to the Bomark motel in the morning and personally take care of the nosy cop. The commander sank back onto the sofa. A short rest would restore him to a state of readiness, then he would prepare for the final strike. The cruise missiles would give them the leverage they needed. In forty-eight hours, he would be out of the country. His eyes felt heavy as he slipped into a restless state, somewhere between sleep and wakefulness. The commander reflected on his past. He had done much since he left the military at age 50. The last ten years had given him complete control over the operation. He never had to get clearance from his superiors but acted under his own volition. It had been better since his departure from the military. There were never any questions and the payments always came like clockwork. His life had changed for the better. He anticipated his retirement to the warm Latin American country. He had already chosen Costa Rica as his destination. He would enjoy the warmth of this tropical haven. It would allow him to savour each day without making detailed plans. His life would become simpler. His retirement cottage was simple in structure, but had been constructed with a high wall to keep the locals separated from the visitors who would come to visit him in his tropical paradise. The commander envisioned a simpler style of life, one which would be free from clandestine activities. His breathing slowed as he found himself drifting into a state of semi-consciousness.

CHAPTER 31

Early morning sounds from the ranch behind the motel awakened Sergeant James. He moved quietly from his bed and walked toward the window. The darkness was slowly lifting as the rays of the early morning sun reached up across the horizon. Detective James attempted to focus on his watch, it was almost five thirty. He dressed quietly as he sat on the bed. He would make another visit to the Hogard ranch. The previous evening he had watched from the roadside, but the van had not returned. Detective James had been tempted to remain on surveillance but without back-up had decided it would not be a wise decision. He had returned to the motel.

He left the Bomark motel and drove in the direction of the abandoned farm house. This wasn't the first time he had worked alone, but it could be his last if he wasn't cautious. As he neared the property, he deactivated the vehicle lights. Sliding from the car seat, he withdrew his holstered weapon from beneath his jacket and slowly made his way down the driveway. As he neared the clearing, he stepped off the roadway and entered the wooded area next to the house. The lights in the building were off. He walked quietly to the shed and looked in. The vehicle had not returned. Walking toward the building, he noticed the back door of the farmhouse slightly ajar. Cautiously, the detective made his way to the door and opened it. Withdrawing the small flashlight from his pocket, he shone the beam into the dark confines of the building, listening carefully as he crept forward. He checked the main floor, then made his way to the basement. Then, he crept up the staircase and looked into each bedroom, as he made his way through the house. From the appearance of the unmade beds, Detective James could sense the suspects had recently been there. He walked down the stairs to the main floor of the farmhouse and walked into the kitchen. Empty beer bottles and fast food containers lined the counter. Detective James studied the items on the counter top, he noticed a crumpled piece of paper lying next to a beer bottle. He reached down and retrieved the paper. Unravelling it he studied the contents. A picture of a military compound with an X was etched onto the yellow parchment. Detective James had been there the day prior and recognized the drawing of the airbase. As he studied the drawing, the plan became clear. The terrorists were going to make an attack on the cruise missile operation. Detective James shoved the crumpled piece of paper into his jacket pocket. He made his way from the building, slamming the door as he left the premises and hurried toward his car. Pushing the pedal to the floor, the vehicle fish-tailed and then accelerated as the detective headed toward the military airbase.

Detective James reflected over the events which had taken place during the last month of the investigation. Jobin had been murdered in his home in Toronto, Milano murdered outside of his office in New York. Emerald Lee had been captured at the scene of the crime but had escaped from Bingham. He had followed Lee and two of the terrorists to Alberta only to learn of a probable attack on the Military base. As he thought about the case, his vehicle sped toward the scene of the impending attack. In the distance he could see the sentry post. Detective James drove up to the building and depressed the brake. He got out of the vehicle and made his way into the building.

"I'm Sergeant James! Is Major Hathaway in?" he asked as he flashed his badge.

"No he isn't! I don't expect him for another fifteen minutes. I can't let you on the base until the major arrives. He is the only one who can give you clearance," said the guard.

"I'll wait in my car," responded the detective as he walked back to his vehicle and got in. He removed his gun from his holster and checked it. As his thoughts raced over the case, he could see headlights of a vehicle in his rear mirror quickly approaching. He released the safety on his automatic weapon and returned it to his holster. A vehicle pulled up to the curb, Major Hathaway got out of his jeep. The major would have to do some fast talking. The commander and his men would be arriving in minutes and pandemonium would take place. He talked to the guard, then returned to his vehicle. He motioned the detective to follow him in the direction of his office. Sergeant James found himself glancing over at the aircraft hangars as he passed the buildings. There wasn't any sign of the white van. Major Hathaway stopped in front of his headquarters, and motioned the detective to follow him. They entered the building, Sergeant James did not see the major's secretary they were alone.

"What brings you to the base at this time of the morning sergeant?" asked the major inquisitively.

"Sir, I have reason to believe this base is going to be attacked by terrorists," he replied.

"Terrorists?" queried Major Hathaway.

"That is correct major. I also have reason to believe they are receiving assistance from someone on this military airbase." Detective James noticed Major Hathaway's complexion change from its ruddy appearance to a pasty grey. The major attempted to withdraw his weapon from his holster. Sergeant James sprang forward and using a combative manoeuvre, delivered a kick at the major's weapon. As his feet made contact with the floor, the cop spun and delivered an elbow to the major's head. Detective James retrieved the major's weapon. He seated the major on a chair and handcuffed him. Removing the phone from the receiver on the desk, he made the 911 call. The dispatcher was asked to send RCMP officers to the airbase.

Sergeant James left the major's office and stealthily made his way toward the hangars. From his position, he could see the white van. The large doors of the hangar had already retracted and two jets rolled forward on the tarmac. The terrorists had advanced their operation, Detective James realized he was too late. In the distance, he could see vehicles with lights flashing, driving toward the military base. They did not stop at the gate, but crashed through the barrier. Sergeant James watched as the two aircraft made their way down the tarmac and lift into the air. Vehicles screeched to a halt in front of him. He heard them yell in unison to drop his weapon. Detective James slowly lowered his gun onto the pavement. With his hands above his head, he waited for the approaching officers. His left hand clutched his badge and he yelled out his operative. The approaching officers inspected his identification and the officer in charge indicated they had received the call on their way to the base.

"I'm Major Henderson, RCMP Special Investigations Unit. We've been working on this one for three months. Major Hathaway has been implicated in treasonous activity. We just saw two aircraft lift off, was the major on them?" asked Major Henderson.

"No sir, I have him handcuffed in his office," replied the detective.

"Radio military! They have got to stop those jets" shouted Major Henderson. RCMP personnel ran forward and entered the military command office. They returned with Major Hathaway still in handcuffs.

"Here are the keys," stated Sergeant James as he tossed them to the RCMP officer. Major Hathaway was slowly coming out of his comatose state. He looked at the officers but said nothing.

"Where are they heading major? You can make it easier on yourself by giving us the information." Major Hathaway said nothing but only stared down at his feet.

CHAPTER 32

"This is P-14 to ground control. Come in please?" said the young pilot.

"Ground control," echoed in his headset.

"I've located one of the aircraft. I just went in for a closer look. There's no one in the cockpit. It must be on automatic pilot. The missiles have been fired," he said. The young pilot listened intently to the command.

"Yes sir! Ready to launch," he responded. The pilot manouvered his Hornet aircraft and circled behind the J-78, then centred on it. His thumb depressed the button. A heat seeking missile shot forward from his jet. Within seconds the J-78 exploded into flames. His instructions were clear, search and destroy. The young pilot dove his sleek F-111 fighter closer to the earth surface. It slid through the cloud cover. It would be only a matter of time before the cruise missiles and the second jet were spotted. They would have to be shot down above deserted land mass. Corporal Best knew the warheads would prove lethal. The young pilot could see the visible tree line. He steered the F-111 over the heavy forested area. Off to his right, he noticed a reflection. He circled back to inspect the area.

"P-14 calling home base. I've just shot down the J-78. Would you like me to continue the search?" asked the pilot.

"No return to home base P-14. They're out of range. One missile was located on radar heading due west toward Seattle. The other is heading in a southwesterly direction. We think it's aimed at Salt Lake City," said the operator.

"I'm coming in! Over and out!" said Corporal Best. He thought back to his days of training in the Pacific. His division had fired nuclear warheads into the ocean. The area had to he cleared for fifty square miles from point of impact. He knew the military couldn't take a chance on a mid-air explosion. Many people would risk death or injury by the ensuing blast. He wondered if the new electronic equipment at the Wyoming base would be useful in re-directing the missiles. Within a mile from the base, Corporal Best radioed the air dispatcher and received instructions to land. As the F-111 touched down, it quickly decelerated. The aircraft glided over the tarmac surface. At the end of the runway, the pilot made a left turn and coasted back to the hangar. He removed his headgear and hurried into the navigation building. A salute was given as he passed his commanding officer. He could feel the tension in the air as he walked into the control room.

"Nice shooting Best," said one of his fellow pilots.

"Thanks! With the new heatseeking rockets it's no bid deal, just aim and fire," he responded.

"Any word about the missiles?" he asked the officer next to him.

"They have spotted one, but can't re-route it. They are waiting to shoot it down when it is over the mountains. Could be some fatalities, we're uncertain how many people are in the vicinity. What about the second one?" he asked.

"It must be flying close to the earth's surface because we haven't sighted it yet. I was just talking to one of the operators at the Wyoming base. He thinks they may be able to re-route the missile, but can't promise anything. The terrorists may have jammed the guidance system. They will have to shoot it down if all else fails. We haven't located the other jet," he said.

"Montana 1 calling Wyoming 11. Come in please?" he said.

"This is Wyoming 11," we have been unsuccessful in re-directing the missile! We are going to have to shoot it down. The second missile has not been located.

CHAPTER 33

Two solitary figures hurried along the dirt road. The commander stared intently at his accomplice.

"I can't believe they would not acquiesce to our demands. They deserve the two missiles coming at them. Emerald, I trust you set the guidance system so they would fly undetected?" the commander asked. Emerald Lee looked over at the commander.

"I sure did boss, just like you told me," he replied. Emerald Lee was finally starting to feel good about himself. He had not only disarmed the devices on the missiles, but had set one on a course for the Pacific. The second missile was programmed to crash into the hilly terrain 100 miles north of Missoula, Montana. Emerald Lee hoped no one would be hurt in the ensuing explosion. By the time his commander discovered the error, he would be gone. Something deep inside his brain had prompted him to react against the grain of terrorism. He wasn't sure how to explain it. His thoughts reflected back to Brenda Williams and Mrs. Pierce. Somewhere deep within his brain, images of people who had treated him kindly bombarded his senses. An overwhelming feeling of well-being surfaced within him. He would have to control his emotions. He did not want the commander to sense his elation. Emerald Lee stared at the commander who was still scowling at his predicament.

The two mercenaries had to parachute from the craft as it lost altitude. Emerald Lee had not only been successful in sabotaging the missiles but had also damaged the engines in the two aircraft. The commander repeatedly cursed Major Hathaway right up to the time they bailed out of the aircraft. Emerald Lee re-assured his commander the missiles were still operable and would destroy their targets. As the trio walked along the dirt road, they turned as the rumble of a truck was heard in the distance.

"There's our ticket out of this place," said the commander. The old truck stopped beside them.

"You fellows going into town?" asked the old grey haired man.

"Yea we are," replied the commander.

"Well hop in," said the old man. The commander opened the passenger door and with one quick motion grabbed the driver from his seat yanking him from the vehicle.

"No need to be so dam hard on me. You can have her he said," as he scurried into the bush. The commander reached for his handgun and aimed it in the old man's direction, but the gun failed to fire.

"Must be his lucky day", said Emerald Lee.

"Shut up Lee or you'll be walking! Let's clear out of here before that old fart recovers his faculties and notifies the authorities," said the commander. He activated the radio and strained his ears, hoping there would be news about the missiles. They'd have to evacuate the cities or face fatalities. The commander continued through the channels but did not get any news of the event.

"Emerald are you sure you wired those jamming devices properly?" he asked.

"I sure did commander! They will certainly find their target. I did my job just the way you told me." Emerald Lee sat quietly in the cab. He knew he'd have to make a break for it. From the way the commander was acting, he'd probably end up dead. Emerald looked over at the gas gauge, the truck was running low on fuel. The commander would soon notice, then they would have to stop for a fill up. Through his peripheral vision, he kept an eye on the commander. If the commander went for his gun, Emerald would be ready. He had been in tighter spots and survived the onslaught. Emerald leaned forward to adjust the laces on his boots. With his right hand, he caressed the metal object strapped to his leg. As he sat up, he could see the Gazron sign in the distance.

"How's the gas commander?" he asked. The commander glanced at the gauge.

"We'd better fill it up," he said. As the vehicle came to a stop, a greasy haired attendant ran out to the truck.

"What'll it be mister?" he asked.

"Fill it!" said the commander.

"Would you like a coffee?" asked Emerald.

"Yea? Black no sugar!" replied the commander.

"I'll be right back," replied Emerald. He walked into the seedy restaurant and ordered two coffee. Emerald asked where the toilet was located? The waitress pointed to a sign. He walked to the rear of the building and entered the washroom. Propping himself on the grimy sink, Emerald raised the window. He could see a wooded area which would provide some cover. Quickly, he slid through the opening and landed on the grassy area beneath the window. Without hesitation, he sprinted the fifty yards separating the building from the cover of the bush. The restaurant was about a mile from town. He would take his direction from the sun and make it there by foot. By the time the commander realized he was gone, it would be too late. Emerald reflected on his plans as he ran through the densely covered bush. He would take a train to the nearest city and then return to New York by bus. He increased his pace and extended his hands in front of his face as he pushed back the saplings blocking his pathway. With the five minute head start, Emerald knew he would gain the distance needed to evade the commander. If everything went according to his plan, he would be back in New York city by tomorrow.

CHAPTER 34

A misty rain sprinkled lightly from the overcast sky. Lieutenant Brown glanced out from his apartment window overlooking the city. A stillness hung in the air. Few cars moved in the streets below. He had received the telephone call from his captain. Lieutenant Brown was provided with the details of the incident at the Cold Lake airbase. From the update, he learned Emerald Lee and his associates had gotten away. The cruise missiles had respectively crashed; one into the Pacific Ocean and the other in the forested area 100 miles north of Missoula, Montana. An APB had been placed across the North American continent. Interpol had been notified about the terrorists. It had been almost a week since the theft of the cruise missiles. Detective Brown had a feeling Emerald Lee would return to New York city. It would just be a matter of time before he caught up with the suspect. As he sat at his table reading the morning newspaper his phone rang.

"This is Captain Smith, I just received a call, a man fitting Emerald Lee's description has been seen in the vicinity of Brenda William's apartment. Our men followed him, but they lost Lee in the subway. This might be the break we need to bring him in," said the captain. Lieutenant Brown put the phone down. He had interrogated Brenda and given her a directive. Turn Lee in when he contacted her, or she was going to prison. Lieutenant Brown was convinced she would cooperate, especially if it meant not spending time in jail. Brenda Williams had been released from custody but was being closely watched by the undercover officers. Detective Brown had a hunch Emerald Lee would attempt to contact her. The detective hurried out to his car. He didn't notice the eyes riveted on him as he opened the car door.

"Crosby keep an eye on him. He has all the details and probably already knows where Lee is hiding. He will lead us to Emerald. Our inside man says they have Lee's girlfriend under surveillance. Emerald is bound to slip up, then we will have him. I have been given orders to terminate Lee," said the dark occupant in the rear seat.

The precinct was busier than usual for a Sunday morning. Like clockwork the criminals got busted on a Saturday night, police officers worked all Sunday to complete the paperwork and by Monday morning their lawyers had them back on the street. The criminal justice system almost seemed pointless to Detective Brown. He had been promised a promotion to captain. He would play it just like Dr. Peterson had told him and not mess up his chances.

Lieutenant Brown knocked on the captain's door, he heard a voice inside asking him to enter. As he opened the door, he acknowledged the mayor sitting next to the captain's desk.

"What's up gentlemen?" he asked.

"An official has put in a good word for you Brown. You are going to receive a commendation for your work on this case. I'm not sure what happened, but it seems Emerald Lee and his associates really screwed this one up," said the captain. Lieutenant Brown thought back to his conversation with Dr. Peterson. She stated Emerald Lee had been nanowired. They had placed a silicon chip in his head and re-wired his neuronal circuitry. The medical intervention likely caused Lee to sabotage the cruise missile operation.

"Good work Brown! I knew you had the situation under control. I've got the commendation typed up and the mayor will be signing it. Congratulations on your promotion to captain of this precinct. Mayor Jefferson is running for Senate and I'll be moving across the street to city hall. I'm taking over as the mayor of New York city", said the captain.

Lieutenant Brown was flabbergasted. It was just as Dr. Peterson had promised. Captain Smith and Mayor Jefferson were definitely part of the movement to re-define the criminal justice system. Detective Brown knew he could never discuss it with them. The Bureau of Corrections and Rehabilitation had probably received the mandate from the new Attorney General. Lieutenant Brown wondered whether the new mandate went all the way up to the Whitehouse? He would leave it for now. It didn't matter who initiated the operative, he would follow the command and would be ready to take control.

Lieutenant Brown had a hunch Brenda Williams would soon be contacting him. This time, he wouldn't take it easy on her unless she provided him with all the details. The mercenaries would likely go after Emerald Lee and in time would take him down. It was a win-win situation either way he looked at it. Detective Brown had arrested Emerald Lee and taken him into custody. The medical experts had nanowired him and used Lee to destroy the cruise missile operation.

Detective Brown liked the changes which would prevail. The experts would use nanowiring to turn the criminals against one another. This was better than the tactical methods he had used in the past. In time, the streets of New York would become safer. The medical experts had commenced their work with the psychopaths and eventually would implement the nanotechnology procedure with all criminals. Anyone who broke the law would face scrutiny. The police officers' job would become easier. Those who joined the force would not be at risk in their pursuit of offenders. Only those who could be trusted would be invited to become part of the new operative. Those who became part of the new crime control model would have to ensure the media never got hold of the information. Otherwise, the reporters would turn the medical experimentation into a nightmare. Detective Brown could only imagine the position the civil rights groups would take on this one.

CHAPTER 35

Emerald Lee had been in hiding since his return to New York city. Time was running out and he would have to make contact with her soon. Tucking the gun into his jacket pocket, he made his way to the street. It was a cold and wet morning and there was little activity in the area. The last time he had attempted to contact her, two unidentified men had followed him into the subway. Emerald Lee knew they would come looking for him. His headaches had gotten worse since his return to New York. He often found himself confused by the overwhelming emotions. At times, he was elated and filled with excitement and at other times despondent and depressed. Emerald wondered whether he had acquired a mood disorder. His thoughts had become complicated since his escape from Bingham. He fought with his emotions and attempted to replace them with visions of his new life in the Caribbean.

Looking down at his watch, Emerald Lee realized it was almost 6:00 p.m. He was slowly edging toward the inner core of the city. People strolled nearby, but he did not look at them. As he glanced across the street, Jim's restaurant appeared through the haze. It would not be a good move to enter the building. Studying the cars in the vicinity of the restaurant, Emerald wondered whether his enemy would charge from the confines of the vehicles. He had attempted to contact Brenda but had been informed by the automated message her number was no longer in service. As he waited, Emerald Lee studied every person who entered and left the restaurant. He glanced up from his newspaper once more and thought he recognized her familiar face. Quickly, he lifted himself from the bench and followed. He had to be sure she wasn't under surveillance, then he would approach her. Brenda Lee did not stop and enter the restaurant but only walked past quickly. Picking up his pace, Emerald hurried after her. He crossed the street and was only a matter of yards behind her. He called out to Brenda but she did not stop. Sprinting ahead, he grabbed at her coat sleeve. Two men looked on as Brenda Williams startled. Their eyes were glued on the attacker but no one moved forward to assist.

"Brenda, why didn't you stop?" he asked.

"I know who you are! Stay away from me! I just can't believe you would do such a thing. Why did you use me?" she asked. The crowd was dispersing. It was just another lover's spat with that same old familiar line. Emerald attempted to calm her down. Placing his hand on her shoulder, he caressed her.

"I never wanted you to find out about this. I got involved with the wrong people. I have left the mercenary group. I've got to leave town, they are after me. I want you to come with me," he said.

"I can't go with you Emerald. Detective Brown interrogated me. I told him I didn't know of your past and didn't have any knowledge of your actions. I must have convinced him, because he released me from jail. The detective told me if he found out I was lying, I was going back to jail. He told me I had to notify him the next time I had contact with you, otherwise I was going to prison for 10 years. I don't have a criminal record, and I don't want one. Emerald please leave me alone and let me go, it is the only way out for me," she said.

"I've done a lot of bad things Brenda, but now it's finished. I didn't go through with the last operation. In fact, I sabotaged it. Something has happened to me. I can't explain it, but I can't bring myself to harm anyone," he blurted.

"I'm sorry Emerald! I love you but I can't take the chance. Lieutenant Brown said I would be indicted and would be convicted for accessory to murder. I just can't live running from the law," she said exasperated by the intensity of the conversation. At first, Emerald was angry with the detective. But the more he thought about his predicament, the more he was angry with himself. Brenda had acknowledged her feelings for him. His narcissism had pushed her away. It wasn't anyone's fault but his own. He could not accept her rejection and wasn't sure he would ever accept his past actions.

"I understand Brenda. It's not your fault, it's mine. I caused this, and now I have to do something about it. I will leave the city but in time will contact you. After you have thought about it, you might change your mind. Keep reading the newspapers, in time the whole story will be leaked to the press. Of all the people I have known in my life, you are the only one I trusted. Forgive me for all the trouble I have caused," he embraced, then released her. Brenda Williams had tears in her eyes as she watched him walk away and fade into the crowd. Emerald got into a yellow cab.

"Where to mister?" the cabbie asked.

"Brady street!" he replied. The cabbie glanced into his rear view mirror as he focused on the occupant in the back seat.

"Do I know you from somewhere," he asked.

"I don't think so. I'm not from New York city," replied Emerald Lee.

"You remind me of someone," said the cabbie.

"I'm not a musician, singer, actor or social worker," replied Emerald. The cabbie didn't answer. He had taxied hookers, pimps and degenerates of all types. He knew it would be best to keep his mouth shut, the guy in the back seat seemed dangerous. Ten minutes passed as they drove the distance to Brady Street.

"This is it! What number did you want?" asked the cabbie.

"This is good, right here. How much do I owe you?" "Thirty-five dollars should cover it," said the cab driver as he combed back his slick black hair. Emerald handed the man two crisp $20.00 dollar bills.

"Keep the change."

"Thanks a lot mister, if you need another ride just ask for Bert Laberre," replied the cab driver.

Emerald got out of the car. He was in a hurry and didn't have any time to worry about change. As he walked along the street, he glanced at the numbers. Emerald located the one he wanted and studied the name plate on the door. He depressed the button beside the name. A lady's voice answered.

"Who is it?" she asked.

"I'm a friend of Max Winter's. Is he in?" asked Emerald.

"Sorry! Max doesn't live here anymore. We had a fight. I'm not sure where he is living," she replied. "Okay", said Emerald. He would return to the old warehouse where he had lived prior to his departure. A plan would have to be made so he could leave the city undetected.

CHAPTER 36

Detective Brown was at the precinct when she called. Brenda Williams provided the details of their encounter and the location where she had talked with him. Detective Brown knew he had scared her during the interrogation, now she was ready to cooperate. Dr. Peterson had mentioned Emerald Lee was no longer a threat because of the silicon implant, but Lieutenant Brown wasn't so sure. According to information filed with his office, two cruise missiles had been fired but the mission had failed because of military intervention. He would give Dr. Peterson another call and then proceed with his final plan to take down the criminal. The detective dialled the cell number she had given him, on the third ring a voice answered.

"This is Lieutenant Brown, I wanted you to know Emerald Lee has returned to New York. A reliable source just called me. You probably haven't heard, but Lee has been linked to a failed cruise missile attack on two American cities. It appears the military discovered the plot and averted the air strike by re-directing the missiles," he said.

"Impossible! The implants were completed successfully. I have gone over the data with the medical team. If Emerald Lee was involved in the missile attack, I believe you will soon discover he had something to do with the failed operation. We re-programmed him! Before you make assumptions about the success of our work, re-evaluate your data. You will likely find some information which confirms the success of our medical intervention," responded Dr. Peterson.

"I know you wanted me to stay away from this one, but I'm going after him. There is an APB on Emerald Lee and police officers are combing the location where he was last seen. I will bring him in. I can't trust the results of your experimentation. Lives could be at stake, and I want to ensure no one gets hurt," said the detective.

"Do what you have to Lieutenant Brown, but I would like to evaluate him after you bring him into custody. I need to know whether the surgery was a success. It will assist us with some answers," she said.

"I can't promise you anything Dr. Peterson. I have informed my men Lee is armed and dangerous. Whatever the outcome, you can review the evidence. If he is killed, I will ensure his body is released to the Bureau of Corrections and Rehabilitation. Then you can probe for the answers," he stated factually.

"Thank-you detective. An autopsy on his brain would provide us with some answers. Then, we would know whether the surgery was a success or a failure," she replied. Lieutenant Brown hung up the phone. He would cooperate with Dr. Peterson and provide the body of the assailant. She had made promises to him which were already reaching fruition. He did not want to ruin his chance for advancement. Either way, he would take over as captain of the precinct. As he contemplated the discussion, Captain Smith marched into his office.

"Any contact yet?" he asked.

"Nothing!" replied Lieutenant Brown.

"I have 100 men combing the area. It is just a matter of time before he is spotted," said Brown. A young rookie rushed into Brown's office.

"Emerald Lee just called, he says he wants to talk to you," blurted the rookie.

"Put him through to my office," replied Brown. Lieutenant Brown waited as the call was transferred. Captain Smith stood nearby as the phone rang.

"Brown speaking."

"This is Lee. For the record, I want you to know Brenda Williams was never involved in any of my operatives. She is an innocent bystander who didn't know of my activities. I know you have interrogated her and tried to shake her down. I want you to leave her alone. If you will give me your word, I'll consider turning myself in," he said.

"I can't make any promises Mr. Lee. You are a wanted man and we can't make any deals. However, if you do turn yourself in, we will go easy on Brenda Williams. You are wanted for a number of homicides and the antic you attempted at the Cold Lake airbase, is a whole other situation. You will get a fair trial but I will be straight up, you'll likely receive the death penalty. Do you understand Mr. Lee?" he stated factually.

"I want to make myself clear Detective Brown. Brenda Williams did not have anything to do with any of this, she is innocent. I will provide testimony on her behalf. I want to surrender," he replied.

"How do you want to go about this Mr. Lee? Are you going to walk into Precinct 14?" he asked snidely.

"I prefer to meet you at a proposed location alone, you can arrest me. It will look better for you, bringing in a suspect of my stature won't it?" Lieutenant Brown could hardly contain his excitement. This was the break he needed. He would be given credit for the arrest. The citizens of New York City would talk highly of him for years to come.

"Okay Mr. Lee, it is a deal. Where will I meet you?" he asked. The detective jotted down the address on his note pad, then hung up the phone.

"What do you think Brown? Do you trust him?" asked the captain.

"He wants me to lay off Brenda Williams. I'm not sure if she was involved. She has a clean record, we have nothing on her. I'm going for the deal. This one will make our precinct look good," said the detective.

"He asked me not to bring anyone. Contact Sergeant Murphy in SWAT, tell him about the situation. Inform him to bring his best snipers and have them posted within 200 yards of our meeting place. I don't want any slip-ups." Lieutenant Brown lifted himself quickly from his chair and bolted for the door. He ran out to his vehicle. With the cruiser light activated, he sped toward the address Emerald Lee had given. As he made his way to the meeting place, Brown could only think of one thing, the promotion. He reflected on the verse he had learned at an earlier time in his career "keep your friends close but your enemies closer". His life would get better. With Lee's arrest, he would no longer have to place his life on the line. The promotion would give him the salary he needed to live a more affluent life. He would re-locate to the suburbs and purchase a home. Life would only get better for him.

As he approached the meeting place, Lieutenant Brown glanced up at the desolate buildings. He seldom visited this section of town unless he was involved in a case. Derelicts lined the sidewalks, their cheap wine camouflaged within brown paper bags. He had seen enough of it when he was growing up in Harlem. He experienced an impulse to career into the wayward vagrants but better judgement prevailed. Adrenalin rushed through his veins and his heart beat rapidly. He wondered whether Emerald Lee would be at the location he had given? The detective pressed the gas pedal to the floor and his car fish tailed as it rounded the corner. Overtaken by adrenalin, Lieutenant Brown didn't notice the black limousine following him in the distance. The building was almost in sight. Just a few more minutes, he thought to himself. He slammed down the brake at the address he was given. From his seat, he glanced up at the building. It could be a trap, he would have to be ready. He made the turn and steered the cruiser to the opposite side of the street. The vantage point would ensure an escape and afford some protection if Emerald had planned an ambush.

From the top window, a pair of eyes riveted on the vehicle. Emerald Lee scanned the area to assure himself the cop had come alone. He could not see any vehicles approaching the area. Emerald would walk out from the building and turn himself in. He opened the window and glanced out at the wary cop. Lieutenant Brown emerged from the vehicle.

"Detective Brown! I'm coming down! I'm not armed," yelled Lee. Lieutenant Brown unholstered his Glock automatic and held it in a downward position. He would be ready just in case this was a trap envisioned by a smart psychopath. Patiently, he waited for the suspect to reach the sidewalk. A door opened on the ground floor. Emerald Lee walked slowly from the building with his hands raised above his head.

"Walk slowly toward me Mr. Lee. I've got you covered," said the wary cop. The suspect walked slowly toward the cop. Lieutenant Brown did not see the eyes focused on him from the building on the opposite side of the street. A 6.5mm Mauser was aimed in his direction, the crosshairs centred on him. A shot rang out, slicing the air and grazing Emerald Lee's right temple before exploding into the pavement. Another shot rang out at the detective as he attempted to return fire. Lieutenant Brown dove behind his vehicle. He watched Emerald Lee clutch at his head and roll quickly for cover behind the parked vehicle. Two more shots rang out at the vehicle where Lee had taken cover. Brown glanced up from his vehicle to pinpoint the location of the rifle fire. He had asked Captain Smith to send in a SWAT team as back-up. Had one of the members of team gone over on him? He wondered who had given the order to fire? He waited as more shots rang out at him and then at Lee. A siren screamed in the distance, Lieutenant Brown looked down the roadway and could see the SWAT vehicle speeding toward them. The tires of the truck came to a screeching halt and four officers in combative dress sprang through the rear doors of the vehicle. Lieutenant Brown looked out from his protected area. He could see Sergeant Murphy on the megaphone shouting the orders. Lieutenant Brown yelled to the commander of the operation someone was on the roof.

The SWAT officers ran into the buildings and vanished from sight. Lieutenant Brown looked up but could not see anyone on the roof top. He crept forward as he made his way to the area where Emerald Lee had taken cover. Traces of blood were splattered on the pavement but there was no sign of Lee. Detective Brown could see the red splatter marks on the pavement, leading up the steps to the building where Emerald Lee had first emerged. Lieutenant Brown ran toward the doorway with his gun drawn. He cautiously opened the door. With his gun in an upright position, he sprinted up the staircase to the upper floor. Blood covered the doorway leading to the roof. Lieutenant Brown moved ever so cautiously to the rooftop expecting to hear the sound of explosive firepower. Looking out from the protection of the building, he scanned the area for snipers. The area was still. He wondered what had happened to the SWAT officers?

Two hundred yards away, the detective did not see the sniper focusing the crosshairs on him. As the sniper fine tuned the Zeus scope, he did not hear a sound but only felt the cold blade slice through his jugular vein. The last sensation the sniper experienced was the numbing in his brain and his vision growing blurry. He slouched to his knees and released the weapon. Glancing slightly over his left shoulder, he stared at Max Winters' lifeless body. Looking upward, he stared at his known assailant.

"I was finished with the operation. You should have left me alone Crosby." Emerald Lee removed the rifle from the sniper's hands. Lieutenant Brown watched as Lee dropped the rifle and walked slowly from the crime scene.

EVALUATION OF THE NOVEL

CLINICAL/FORENSIC QUESTIONS

CHAPTER 1:
1) Describe what is meant by Crime Scene Analysis?
2) Utilize the Turvey Model of Crime Scene analysis to evaluate the techniques a Forensic Team would use in their investigation?

CHAPTER 2:
1) In this chapter one gets a glimpse into the private world of Emerald Lee.
   a) Utilize the Nature versus Nurture debate to describe reasons for his behavioural problems.
   b) Mr. Lee makes a statement "what kind of cruel bastard would shoot a pigeon anyway?" then a few minutes later executes a businessman. Discuss the reasoning process of psychopaths.
   c) What defense mechanisms does Emerald Lee use?
   d) Is Emerald Lee's psychopathology commensurate with biological disorder or psychological disorder?
   e) Name Emerald Lee's disorder.

CHAPTER 3:
1) What type of man is Lieutenant Brown? Provide a tentative psychological profile?
2) Post-traumatic stress disorder was a common problem amongst soldiers following war.
   a) Describe the characteristics of this syndrome?
   b) Does Lieutenant Brown appear to suffer from this disorder? Describe some of his symptoms.
3) Utilize learning theory (ie. conditioning)   todescribe the causation of post-traumatic stress disorder?

CHAPTER 4:
1) Sex offenders are a deviant group with underlying pathology. Utilize research models to describe the basis of this disorder?
2) Are sex offenders (ie. rapists, child molesters, incestuous and pedophiles)   alike or do they possess characteristics which separate them into different groups?
3) Describe the research of Marshall, Record, Barbaree, Valliant and others regarding sex offenders (ie. psychological profile).

CHAPTER 5:
1) Define the following:
   a) Modus Operandus
   b) Motive
   c) Criminal Intent
   d) CPIC File
2) Is George Blundel justified in his use of tactical devices to stop the terrorists from harming Jonathan Richardson?

CHAPTER 6:

1) Describe the psychological profile of terrorists?
2) Are mercenary terrorists any different than religious terrorists? Provide the psychological profile of both groups?
3) Are all terrorists psychopathic?
4) Describe the stressors police officers have to contend with on the job.

CHAPTER 7:

1) Describe the differences between a psychotic homicidal killer and a professional contract killer? Why is Emerald Lee's personality more consistent with that of the contract killer?
2) What is "bystander apathy" (Latane and Darley)?
3) Why did the bombing of the Twin Towers cause the USA to change their philosophy on their immigration policy?
4) Who is Konrad Lorenz? What is his theory on aggression?
5) Who is Eibl-Eibesfeldt? What is his theory on territorial behaviour?
6) Who is R. Ardrey? What did he state about the territorial imperative?
7) How does "eye contact" lead to aggression in the animal and human kingdom? Discuss Detective Brown's view on eye contact and aggression.
8) Why should criminals (ie. people, property, and sexual offenders) be segregated in prison?
9) Define:
   a) Mens Rea
   b) Actus Reus
   c) Judicial Order (30, 60, 90)
   d) Warrant of the Lieutenant General

CHAPTER 8:
1) Who was Egas Moniz? What was the purpose of his brain surgery?
2) What is frontal lobotomy?
3) Why was frontal lobotomy used?
4) Why does Emerald Lee believe brain surgery is taking place at the Bingham Neurosurgical Centre?
5) What is the purpose of Forensic Units in psychiatric hospitals?

CHAPTER 9:
1) Define the following:
   a) Terrorists
   b) Terrorism
2) Name and describe the types of terrorists?
3) What is the commonality between terrorists?
4) Can terrorists be treated/re-conditioned?
5) How do anti-terrorist squads capture terrorists?

CHAPTER 10:
1) Why are forensic psychological assessments conducted on people who commit violent offenses?
2) Why should psychologists perform intellectual /cognitive evaluation prior to other psychometric tests? What information does the Wechsler provide?
3) Why is personality assessment important to the forensic evaluation?
4) Describe the differences between the Rorschach Projective Ink Blot test and the Minnesota Multiphasic Personality Inventory?
5) What information is provided by the aforementioned tests?
6) Which clinical scales would be elevated on the MMPI for Emerald Lee?

7) Robert Heath of Tulane University conducted electrode implantation in brains of prisoners. What did he and his colleagues hope to achieve?

8) Why was brain experimental research funded by the CIA? What did they expect to accomplish with the results of their research?

CHAPTER 11:

1) Are forensic investigations of suspects in the "field" any different from forensic evaluations in controlled interview rooms?

2) Police officers who perform surveillance must use specified methods in order to carry out their operations. Name some of these techniques.

3) Discuss acceptable interrogation techniques used to extract confessions, according to the book "Criminal Interrogations" by Inbau, Reid, Buckley and Jayne.

CHAPTER 12:

1) Why was Homeland Security created in the USA?

2) CSIS operates in Canada as the national security agency.
   a) What are the functions of this security group?
   b) What qualifications does one need to obtain employment with this agency?

3) Are the techniques used at CSIS any different from those used by police officers?

4) What screening must be done of candidates prior to obtaining employment with policing agencies (municipal, provincial, national)?

CHAPTER 13:

1) Dr. Allen provides a synopsis of Emerald Lee. According to the information, Emerald Lee had been physically abused by his mother's boyfriend. Furthermore, he was emotionally abandoned by his mother. How does an unstable childhood lead to later character disorder?

2) What is a court ordered assessment?

3) Why does the court request 30, 60 or 90 day judicial orders?

4) How do judicial orders differ from the Warrant of the Lieutenant Governor?

5) What is psychopathic disorder?

6) Name and describe the different types of psychopaths.

7) Describe the views of prominent theorists (Gough, Quay, Doren, Quinsey, Valliant) regarding underlying features that lead to psychopathic personality?

8) Lt. Brown seems oblivious to the information which Homeland Security, the FBI and the RCMP have on Emerald Lee. Why do police agencies seldomly share information with other police agencies? What are the advantages and disadvantages of this method of operation?

CHAPTER 14:

1) Emerald Lee does not get along with patients or staff. He believes that he must manipulate others. Discuss the basis of Emerald Lee's character disorder.

2) Why is it difficult to treat psychopaths?

3) What have some (Valliant, Quinsey, Rice) found in their research with psychopaths?

4) Do psychopaths possess moral reasoning? If they do, why are they unable to utilize moral reasoning?

CHAPTER 15:

1) Knowing that behaviour is predictable should enable Dr. Allen and Lieutenant Brown to formulate plans to capture Emerald Lee. Name these behaviours?

2) As a student of Forensic Psychology what plans would you attempt to implement in order to capture a criminal?

3) In his article "Predicting Violent Behavior", John Monaghan discusses the advent of predictability of behavior.
   a) Discuss the personality and motivational factors implicit in the predictability model?
   b) Discuss the role of weapons and victims in this model?

4) What is an impulsive psychopath? Is Emerald Lee an impulsive psychopath? Support you answer with data. 5) Which theorist made the statement "Past Behaviour can Predict Future Behaviour?" Is Emerald Lee's behaviour predictable?

6) Describe the Hare Psychopathy Checklist? Why is this questionnaire useful in the evaluation of offenders?

7) If one were to implement the Hare Psychopathy Checklist with Emerald Lee describe background information which would be of interest to a psychologist?

8) Who was Jose Delgado? What was the basis of his research?

9) Early experimentation in the 1960's evaluated ESB (electrical stimulation of the brain) and lesioning.
   a) Why was this research terminated?
   b) How might ESB and lesioning experimentation be used as a research tool?
   c) Discuss why nanotechnology could be useful with offender populations?
   d) Is the implementation of nanowiring a plausible technique in the treatment of aggressive psychopaths?

CHAPTER 16:

1) Emerald Lee has a rigid view of life. He views others (ie. bohemians and derelicts) with contempt. What does this indicate about the myopic views of psychopathic personality disorder?

CHAPTER 17:

1) In this chapter we are introduced to Brenda Williams. Accordingly, one learns that she has had a relationship with Emerald Lee but never suspected his true profession nor was she aware of his psychopathic personality style. According to Hervey Cleckley in his book "The Mask of Sanity" psychopaths don't have close emotional relationships. Provide some reasons to explain Emerald Lee's involvement with Brenda Williams?

2) Name and describe Hervey Cleckley's traits depicting psychopaths.

CHAPTER 18:

1) Eye witness identification has always been a concern in the investigation process. Describe some of the findings Elizabeth Loftus has noted from her research?

2) In this chapter we are drawn into the world of eyewitness identification.
   a) How detailed was the description given by Mr. Lugani of the suspect Emerald Lee.
   b) What factors can interfere with eye witness identification?
   c) Describe the research by Robert Buckout and his colleagues on "emotionality and eye witness accounts".

CHAPTER 19:

1) Describe the following:
   a) suspicion
   b) paranoia
   c) paranoid personality disorder
   d) paranoid psychoses
2) Does Emerald Lee show signs of paranoid personality? Describe the characteristics?
3) Name the psychometric test(s) used to diagnose paranoid personality?

CHAPTER 20:

1) Emerald Lee recalls a vivid experience of childhood abuse. Describe the experience and comment on the impact of dysfunctional childhood on later adult development?
2) Name and describe five disorders found in later adult development which are attributed to problems during childhood?
3) Can conduct disorder in adolescence and psychopathic disorder in adulthood be a result of dysfunctional behaviour experienced during one's formative development? Explain the causative mechanisms utilizing the research of Doren, Gough and others?
4) Describe the biological models of Hare and Eysenck and the underlying mechanisms attributed to psychopathic disorder?

CHAPTER 21:

1) What is psychiatric (mental) illness?
2) Why does Emerald Lee not understand the difference between psychiatric illness and his disorder?

CHAPTER 22:

1) Describe the techniques police officers use during an investigative procedure?
2) What is the role of the Forensic Investigative unit?
3) Describe the nature of the work each forensic individual performs in the evaluation of crime scenes?
4) During forensic evaluation of crime scenes every piece of information must be assembled to provide a profile of the crime as well as the perpetrator.
   a) Name and describe some of the evidence used in this process.
   b) Why does Sergeant James believe "charred remains" of a map would be useful in his investi- gation?

CHAPTER 23:

1) Discuss the PET findings obtained by Robert Hare in his research on psychopaths.
2) What other neurological techniques would be useful in evaluating criminal offenders?
3) In the film "A Clockwork Orange - by Stanley Kubrick" one learns that a violent sexual psychopath could be re-programmed with the administration of drugs and classical conditioning. Discuss this aversive model of conditioning and its early use in penal institutions?

CHAPTER 24:

1) Name the percentage of police officers who become "bad cops"?
2) What are the underlying personality characteristics of bad cops?

CHAPTER 25:

1) During interrogation which techniques will Lieuten- ant Brown use on Brenda Williams?
2) What type of interrogation techniques cannot be used with suspects?

CHAPTER 26:

1) During an investigation, police officers often act on hunches. Forensic psychologists also use the concept of hunches in their evaluation (ie. experimental method; hypothesis testing - null versus the alternate). How might police investigation attempt to utilize the scientific method as a measure to evaluate crime scenes?

2) Discuss the deductive versus inductive reasoning models (espoused by B. Turvey) as a method of evaluating crimes?

3) Comment on which techniques are most useful in crime evaluation?

4) What techniques does Detective James seem to be using?

CHAPTER 27:

1) Why do people dream?
   a) Physiological Reason
   b) Psychological Reason

2) Discuss the underlying content of dreams according to Sigmund Freud?
   a) Manifest Content
   b) Latent Content

3) What is an anxiety attack?

4) What is a panic attack?

5) Describe the biological (neurochemical) mechanisms involved in brainstem activation during an anxiety and/or panic attack. Include the role of the RFB, locus coeruleus, and basolateral nucleus of the amygdala?

6) What are some of the factors which would indicate Emerald Lee has been successfully nanowired?

CHAPTER 28:

1) Why do people become angry? (biological, and social factors)?
2) Discuss the biological (neurochemical) bases of anger?
3) What is a passive aggressive personality disorder according to Theodore Millon?
4) Does Major Hathaway appear to suffer from a disorder? Describe the characteristics of his disorder.

CHAPTER 29:

1) Police officers must be cautious when they undertake investigations. Discuss personal characteristics which would ensure a police officer's safety during a criminal investigation?

CHAPTER 30:

1) In this chapter one obtains a psychological perspective of the «commander». He seems to have multiple aspects to his personality. He functions as a psychopath and an opportunist. However, he is also seen in an earlier chapter risking his life to save his son.
   a) Comment on the multiple roles that people utilize in their everyday functioning.
   b) What is the difference between role playing and multiple personality disorder?
   c) Why do people use defense mechanisms in their everyday behaviour?

CHAPTER 31:

1) In hand to hand combat, which techniques are most useful to police officers? (Don't discuss fire arms).
2) What is the origin of martial art techniques?
3) Comment on the Chinese philosophy of "Yin and Yang".

CHAPTER 32:
1) Discuss the physics of "heat seeking" missiles and their method of operation?
2) Why did the US military develop the cruise missile?

CHAPTER 33:
1) What is nanotechnology?
2) Why was nanotechnology created?
3) Is there a possibility, nanotechnology could be implemented as an alternative to "traditional medi- cine" in the treatment of mental disorder?
4) Could "nanowiring" be used to control aggressive or impulsive psychopaths? Comment on the use of this technique as a way of controlling aggressive psychopaths like Emerald Lee.
5) Describe the logistics in the implementation of nanowiring? (ie. stereotaxic procedures, silicon chip implantation, wiring of neural circuitry)?

CHAPTER 34:
1) Should convicted offenders have rights? Why or why not?
2) Should medical techniques (ie. pharmaceuticals, surgery, nanowiring) be used to control incarcerated offenders or those on probation/parole?
3) Should psychological techniques (ie. classical conditioning, aversive conditioning) be used to control incarcerated offenders or those on probation/parole?
4) What corrective techniques should be used on offenders to protect society from becoming victims?

CHAPTER 35:
1) What are mood disorders?
    a) Describe unipolar?
    b) Describe bipolar?
2) Can mood disorders lead one to commit crimes?
3) What are the best treatments for mood disorders?

CHAPTER 36:
1) What medical data was extracted from the autopsy of Charles Whitman's brain following the Texas University massacre?
2) What information can neuroscientists gain from autopsy?